FATAL DREAMS

A complex yet savory dark, psychological thriller with plenty of meat to the bone—well worth digesting.

Compelling commercial fiction: the intimacy of children, the twisted obsession of a fiend, and the revelation of secrets to a protagonist desperate for the truth.

An alluring visual odyssey that propels the reader through a wistful idealist's poignant, soul-searching probe of his childhood through middle age as he grapples with mystery, murder, mayhem, and his fixation with his past and classic movies.

From nostalgic bestsellers to jukebox oldies, ties to the past are a haven from life's stress. Fatal Dreams, which explores children's lives in the 1960s, their fate as adults, and one child's inexorable psychosis, appeals to those who cherish escapism and are intrigued by psychotic killers.

To Penny,
Hope you like the read!
Drew Lambeth
Lenhoff

FATAL DREAMS

12-6-13

* * *

FATAL DREAMS

DREW LANDRETH

**CDTL
PRESS**

Published by CDTL Press

Front cover: from a painting by Elizabeth 'Buffy' Mechling
Back cover photo (for print version): by Drew Landreth

ISBN-13: 9781537285450
ISBN-10: 1537285459

To dreamers . . .

FATAL DREAMS

Chapter 1

"Damn!" Azoo bolted from the convertible and dashed past the dead end into the woods. He was pumped and paranoid, not just because he had toked too much. His gut churned to the livid shouts from his buddies.

"He fucked up again, big time!" Naylor shook his fists with a grim smirk as he hopped from the bucket seat of the passenger's side onto the asphalt of Latham Street.

"What?" Bish zipped up his fly and whirled around to the gleam of his brother's new 1967 Nantucket blue Corvair Monza. "Where the hell is he going?"

"He burned a hole in the upholstery as big as a freaking Chee•to."

"Shithead!" Bish screamed as he and Naylor tore after Azoo. "Your ass is grass and I'm the lawn mower! When my brother gets wind, if there's anything left after I stomp you, you'll really be begging for mercy."

Through the crisp October air, beneath a shimmering moon, Addison Zooder, dubbed Azoo by Bish, scrambled along the ridge of the creek bank; his corduroy bellbottoms lashed the faded weeds as his frazzled eyes probed for the right spot to dart to the other side. The buzz from the Waheekan Gold bloated his brain: everything glowed and pulsated; his heart thumped like a war hungry howitzer. Thoughts of what Bish was sure to do fanned Azoo's angst. They were catching up. Why was he the slowest? Just rotten luck that Bish was one of Hammond High's varsity runners.

"Finally." Azoo clenched his teeth as he spotted the trail of stepping stones. Skidding down the bank onto the damp earth towards the first rock, he failed to notice the bait and tackle bag. "Damn it!" He grunted and tripped; so much for his new desert boots. The fisherman's bag broke his fall, but it knocked the wind out of him. As he gasped for air his right hand tingled. "Ah!" He shook the wriggling night crawler from his palm and spastically dusted himself from head to toe. Yards away the silhouettes of his fuming cohorts loomed. Holding his breath he prayed that they wouldn't spot him.

Bish shook his finger. "There! I knew I'd find him. Hurry, Naylor, you don't want to miss this."

Azoo shot up and accidentally kicked the bag. As he started across the creek, he turned and glimpsed the eyes from the stumpy mass that had barreled from the rubbery pouch and sat upright in the sandy dirt. "Aaahhhhh!" His startled cry boomed from the woods through the quiet streets of Seminary Valley. Jolted by shock that overshadowed his fear of Bish's revenge, Azoo clutched his throat with his hands.

"Motherfucker!" Bish cocked his fists as he leaped to the floor of the bank. "It's pulverizing time."

"Wait! Bish, for Christ's sake, look!" Azoo was hyperventilating.

"None of your excuses, prickface." He yanked Azoo from the edge of the creek and jabbed him in the chest.

"Hold it!" Naylor jerked Bish around. Seriously, check it out. Azoo isn't kidding; look down—there!"

Bish elbowed Naylor and peered at the thing that seemed to peer back. Azoo whimpered as the grotesque image swelled in his head.

"Holy shit; you know what that is?" Bish cringed as he smacked Azoo in the gut. "Stop thinking about it or you'll never stop crying. God, this is serious! Whoever did this is really sick." Bish marched to it and crouched in wonder. "It has to be real," he tapped its hair, "sure feels real. Naylor, get me a branch."

Like a pulsating jellyfish the severed head glistened in the moonlight.

"Here." Naylor handed his best friend a sopping twig.

Bish poked its forehead and ears, then, between the limp lips, parted its pearly teeth.

"Look," Naylor hunched beside Bish and pointed. "It's like thread or fishing line, stitching—someone's needlework."

Strands of black twine formed a dotted circle on the skin around the lips.

"That is weird." Bish shook his head and chucked the stick in the creek. "It looks like a gigantic shrunken head. God, I wonder who it is; I wonder who the hell did this."

Gazing at the moon Azoo slowly calmed down. He glanced at Bish who seemed to be contemplating what to do. Naylor beamed in utter fascination:

"A real head—freaking boss! Looks fresh to me. See how glassy the eyes are? Unbelievably cool." With a perverted chuckle Naylor rubbed his palms together.

"God!" Bish shoved him. "You're a morbid mother. I swear you give me the creeps. If you weren't my best friend—what are you doing?"

"Leave it alone." Azoo moaned as he forced the grisly image from his thoughts.

"Eat me!" Naylor glared, yanked out a Winston, propped the teeth ajar with his pinky, and slipped the cigarette in. "There, now it looks more dignified, right Bish?"

"Enough, Naylor; stop playing with it. We need to book, now!"

"Just a minute. You know," Naylor grinned, "the face on the head kind of reminds me of Ed Sullivan . . . underwater. Yeah, that's it! And there," he pointed to the fat beetle perched on the chin.

"Man, straighten up!" Bish shook his fist.

"Imagine." Naylor pretended he was Sullivan in front of the CBS cameras presenting the show's most famous star of stars.

He crossed his arms and pursed his lips. "And now, ladies and gentlemen, I know you've all been waiting for this next act. They're here to entertain you twice this evening. These talented lads have flown all the way from Liverpool. And so, without further introduction, here they are," Naylor tucked his middle finger under his thumb placing it half an inch from the beetle, "the Beatles!" He flicked the bug into the creek and roared with laughter.

"That's it!" Bish snatched the cigarette from the mouth of the head and chucked it at Naylor. "We're out of here—now."

"Bish!" Azoo yelped. "You forgot something."

"Yeah, to beat the shit out of you; and when I'm less burnt out, I will."

Azoo squinted. "We need to report this, at least phone the police."

"You," Naylor snorted, "not only look like a zoo, you think like one."

Bish shook Azoo. "Are you tripping? Can you picture us explaining this to the cops now? I can imagine their questions: like how we happened to stumble upon the head, or who we think might have put it there; and don't forget about being stoned: I'm sure the three of us would love to get harassed for that, not to mention that I'm cruising with a driver's permit, not accompanied by an adult, licensed driver—sorry but neither of you qualify. If we contact them, it'll be tomorrow."

Naylor shook his head. "If I could just take it home and find a way to preserve it: what an awesome conversation piece."

"Naylor, you're a maniac; where do you get your demented notions? Forget the head; let's boogie."

Azoo tapped Bish. "We should put it back . . . in that." He pointed to the bait and tackle bag. "After tripping over the pouch I accidentally kicked the head out of it."

"Who the fuck cares." Naylor snapped.

Snatching the waterlogged sack Bish glanced at the inscription, R & J, on the front. "Wonder what that stands for."

Naylor shrugged. "R.J. Reynolds Tobacco Company, or how 'bout Run and Jump, or I know, Runt and Jerkoff, which is Azoo's middle and last name."

"Fuck you!" Azoo scowled, ready to pounce.

"I'll show you who gets fucked!" Naylor swung at Azoo.

"Chill out." Bish's palm caught Naylor's fist.

"Someone needs to put the head in the bag." Azoo kicked the ground.

"I ought to stuff you in the bag." Bish jabbed him. "But since you found it, you can put it back."

"I can't even look at it."

"Hell, I'll do it, chickenshits." Naylor reached over.

"Stop!" Bish waived as if he were conducting an orchestra. "If we report it tomorrow, the police are sure to want things exactly as we left them, not as they were before we found them. I've seen enough 'Perry Mason' and 'Dragnet' episodes to know that."

"Screw it. Let me take it home; come on Bish, who's gonna know?"

"Are you insane?"

"Shh!" Azoo whispered. "Sounds like someone's coming."

"Quiet." Bish growled.

They listened, but nothing.

"I swear I heard someone." Azoo shook his head, sure that the rustling of branches was more than just the wind.

"It's the pot screwing your head. Let's roll." Bish waved.

As they ran from the woods, Bish booted Azoo in the ass. "Don't forget, you owe me for the cost to fix the hole in my brother's car seat."

Chapter 2

Tim gazed into the deepening twilight. It was as if an indigo veil enveloped his face. They were up too high to make out anything below. Not too many passengers: this made the cabin noise faint and surreal, like whispers from flickering spirits. Some teen in the next aisle was grooving to "Kryptonite." For a moment Tim unfurled, his mind a tipsy vagabond. Scenes from the new release, *Almost Famous*, which he saw last Saturday, beckoned . . . sweet siren Kate Hudson with rock group Stillwater and a baby-face Rolling Stone journalist: all on the tour bus singing to "Tiny Dancer." But it was August's news that jolted him back to her. Two months ago classic movie hall-of-famers Alec Guinness and Loretta Young had died, a week apart. Cocking his head he thanked the attendant for drink number two, sipped, and murmured, "Sheri!" He couldn't stop obsessing. The pilot announced they'd be landing at Reagan National in a few hours.

Tim Carol, a successful commercial real estate appraiser, had made Seattle his home for decades. From his downtown office he and his partner valued everything from strip centers and high-rise offices to cemeteries. Tim also traveled the country teaching appraisal. That's what awaited him in the nation's capital.

Rubbing his palms together he pictured his old neighborhood in Northern Virginia, so close to D.C. He'd have to revisit if he had time. "But Sheri," his lips twitched, "she can't be dead!"

Sheri Riddick, Tim's childhood sweetheart, was a skinny tomboy. Softhearted and good-natured, her effervescent spirit was accentuated by emerald-green eyes and a Shirley Temple haircut. Sheri and Tim loved classic movies, TV, swimming, bicycling, board games, and ghost stories, including the ones they told each other when the time was right; that plus an undeniable attraction made them inseparable.

In the '60s, Seminary Valley, a middle-class suburb of Alexandria, Virginia, was new and fresh: the streets were smooth and wide, the sidewalks were clean and bright, the trees and shrubs were young and fit, and almost everyone took pride in his or her yard. This enhanced the natural high kids were on.

Tim pictured his childhood in seasons:

Winter meant sledding and snow forts; hide-and-seek in the frosty air; comic books beside a blazing hearth; board games like Risk, Broadside, and Hands Down; cutting thru backyards at dusk while gazing into illuminated rec. rooms where neighbors sometimes moved, though their voices were seldom heard; grinning with wide eyes at the threads of popcorn wound 'round the Christmas tree; and being lulled to sleep by the tipsy voices of his parent's New Year's Eve guests.

With spring came Easter egg hunts; the velvety grass bursting with daisies, buttercups, and clover, irresistible for skidding and sliding on until his jeans were green at the knees; testing strange concoctions with his chemistry set as rain spattered the basement windows; and hopping the backyard fence—his palms slick with the morning dew—to run to the adjoining cul-de-sac in hopes of winning at marbles.

In summer he loved kickball, wiffle ball, grass fights, and "chicken" fights; pawing the silver change in his palm making sure it was enough for the ice cream man; and on hot nights peering at the double-Ferris wheel from the carnival on the bluff overlooking his neighborhood, a dazzling parade of color and light that captivated Tim's heart like his first glimpse of the Emerald City of Oz.

Fall provided new classmates, tackle football, Halloween costumes and honey-colored turkey; twirling in headlocks with playmates over the earthy grass; whiffs of glue and paint he used to create his favorite monster models, which his mother hated; and wistfully gazing out his classroom window at the autumn trees wishing he were Hollywood swashbuckler Errol Flynn dueling a wicked count over the honor of a radiant maiden, or TV secret agent Napoleon Solo—the man from U.N.C.L.E.—pitting his life and wits against THRUSH, the diabolical global enemy, or any of the Beatles on stage exciting countless adoring fans.

Sheri and Tim were children for much of the 1960's—an intense, passionate decade when so many starry-eyed baby-boomers shuddered at the thought of growing up or old. Their idols inspired them to believe that they had the power to change the world; they were the keepers of the eternal flame. It's funny how so few of that generation could foresee how hard their dreams would come crashing down.

Somewhere between the naive '50s and the volatile '60s America's innocence was eclipsed by a new strain of reasoning and a new monster to cultivate it. The distant threat of aliens and communism gave way to a more tangible, intimate menace. From murders and assassinations at home and around the globe to books like *In Cold Blood* and films like *Psycho*: millions of people were affected, some permanently scarred. It was as if in the distance you could sense hundreds of closet doors creaking open and the suppressed snickers from the psychopaths as they slithered out. You weren't sure whether the killer in the news lived 500 miles away or next-door; and murder, it seemed, didn't have a reason; and getting to sleep was tougher than it used to be. Many tried to ignore the thought of waking up in the middle of the night face to face with a maniac. The only monsters in Sheri and Tim's world were movie fiends like Frankenstein, Dracula, and the Wolfman who they were sure lived somewhere nearby. Little did they know that real monsters lurked in the shadows. Tim would never understand those freaks or their motives. If there was only a way to make them vanish!

He smiled as she beckoned to him. Her beauty enthralled his senses. He'd give anything to be with her. Like multicolored wildflowers whirling in an autumn breeze, she stirred his soul; like a cool spritzer on a steamy afternoon, her radiant eyes quenched his longing; like a heavenly mist her tender voice caressed his heart: Sheri! Tim pictured her as a nine-year-old who gazed at him as if she were waiting patiently for her favorite dessert. He was ten . . .

Wheeling his year-old Huffy from the shed, Tim scrambled around front to wait for her, but there she was waiting for him.

"Come on!" She stomped the ground. "We haven't much time."

"What's the hurry?"

"Mom." Sheri shook her head. "She wants me back in two hours. She has a list of errands she needs me to run. I'm sorry I yelled at you. It's just that every time I want to have fun, something always screws it up."

"That's okay." Tim peered into her frazzled eyes and tried to pump a smile out of her as he hopped around on the hot concrete. He was in too much of a hurry to slip on his tennis shoes. "Two hours is fine. Let's roll," he motioned. Tim sensed her mood brighten. He knew they were minutes away from having a blast. "What about Honey?" He frowned. "I can picture her at the pool, poking her nose in the chain-link fence, whining for us to let her in."

"Don't worry, Mom promised to keep her inside for at least 20 minutes. That'll give us plenty of time."

They peddled up the smooth asphalt. The sun, a roaring blaze, beamed against their shoulders. Tim's ocean-blue swimming trunks sagged; his towel was knotted around his handlebars. They were neck and neck. She was always able to keep pace—a beacon of stamina. Tim marveled at how nicely Sheri's swimsuit highlighted her mellow skin and how the dangling charms of her new bracelet glittered like choice crystal. As she pumped with ease on her Schwinn, the towel draped 'round her fluttered like a Roman cape. They were nearing the pool: their first real time alone together. It was the summer of '66, and Tim reeled with infatuation—new, fresh, and innocent, call it first love; yet it was as real and moving as any he would ever experience: a love that would burn in him for a lifetime.

"Here." She motioned as they fishtailed onto the gravel in front of the clubhouse. Sheri handed Tim three morsels.

He popped two in his mouth and hopped from his bike.

"Aren't you going to look?" She shoved him.

Tim squinted at the last bit in his palm, a piece of chalk-purple valentine candy with the words BE MINE in pink. His face turned as red as the sunburn he would feel that night. His heart tingled as he thanked her.

Racing past the front desk Tim was blinded as he bolted from the men's room. He pitched a hand to his eyebrows and sighed at the motley crowd that dotted the grounds like sprinkles on vanilla ice cream and at the two gigantic, glistening, mint-mouthwash blue pools. Daydreaming to the reflections, one of Tim's favorites blared from the clubhouse PA. It fit his mood perfectly. Clanging guitars, mounting drums, and John's smashing vocal ignited "Eight Days a Week." Tim glanced to his left and grinned. Sheri had just exited the clubhouse. What perfect timing. Casually she nodded at the boards. With a sleek jackknife she popped the air and sliced the water. He surged up the high dive pretending he was a GI bursting from a trench. Stomping onto the platform he nodded at the horizon. "I'm as free as the wind."

"What are you waiting for, the next century?" someone shouted.

Tim skipped to the end and kicked out into a preacher position. Plummeting through the air his legs and butt clapped the water scattering it like shrapnel. Underwater he gazed at the bubbles and bodies and laughed hysterically.

Shouts and splashes echoed as he and Sheri traipsed up the slope. Near the crest they settled in the shade of a tall tulip tree where they devoured their snacks. The fragrance of honeysuckle sweetened the air.

"Hear it?" She motioned.

The last bite of Tim's hot dog slid through his fingers and tumbled to the parched grass. Lounging shoulder to shoulder they beamed. From the tinny sounding clubhouse speakers, minstrel guitars and soulful voices brought smiles and goose bumps. The first time Tim and Sheri heard "Bus Stop," they knew it was amazing. Holding hands they closed their eyes as the bittersweet ballad eclipsed time exalting their hearts and minds. They whispered the lyrics to the second half of the chorus: their favorite part of the song . . .

As "Bus Stop" faded they rode the moment until a plum speckled butterfly fluttered by.

"Have some, half of mine is left." Tim glimpsed her empty bottle.

Sharing the soda as their parents would a bottle of vintage wine, they smiled and toasted the day.

Sheri edged her towel into the sunlight. "Put yours next to mine; I'll get tan while you stay cool." She squeezed a pearl drop of Coppertone into her palm and gently massaged her legs.

Tim smiled as he imagined.

"When you get older what do you want to be?" Her melodic voice parted his trance.

"An archeologist," Tim pointed to the east. "Wouldn't it be cool to fly to Egypt dressed in official khakis and a pith helmet, in search of the remains of one of the great kings? Can't you picture entering the tomb, all the gold and jewels glittering?"

"I wouldn't mind Egypt," she winked, "if I was with the right person."

"There's something I'd like more." Tim gazed at her with longing. "Imagine I'm a scientist, like Spencer Tracy as Dr. Jekyll, with test tubes brimming and beakers bubbling, probing the secrets of life."

"Not to mention the fringe benefits: you know, Lana Turner and Ingrid Bergman."

Tim stared at the grass and stifled a grin. "It'd be great to make important discoveries—how about you?"

"Soaring above the clouds as a pilot, helping people safely reach their destination—that's my idea of a great job; or caring for the sick: if I were a doctor or nurse, I'd treat all my patients like family."

Tim pictured her in soft, white linen stroking his head and asking if there was anything he needed.

"Ever wonder about marriage and children?" Her eyes skimmed the soft horizon. "If you were a scientist and I were a doctor, we'd make sure that our work didn't interfere with being together or being with our kids."

Tim thoughts flitted to a peculiar playmate they had met the previous fall. From time to time Tim worried about him: an only child who spent most of his limited playtime with Tim and Sheri; he considered them his only friends. His mood swings from hyper to hush were quick and sure like the swish of a slick pendulum. He *was* strange, not just because he loved bologna sandwiches with ketchup and mustard, or that he walked around half-naked in winter and cloaked in summer—no, there were other, eerie quirks: like the time he showed up with homemade voodoo dolls pretending they were his parents. Giggling nervously with oversized sewing needles, he speared each pillowy creation while murmuring a witch doctor's hex. Strange as it seemed, for a week his father was sick with a bizarre stomach ailment. Tim and Sheri were convinced he had extraordinary powers.

"I wonder about Robert." Tim blurted.

Sheri cringed. "Everything was perfect until now."

Large chestnut eyes hinted at his melancholy; soft raven hair highlighted his pale complexion. He was proud of his early-Beatles haircut, even if Tim and Sheri agreed it looked more like Moe's of the Three Stooges.

Although they were fascinated with Robert and his weird tales, he often made Sheri nervous. Robert believed she was secretly attracted to him; Sheri was just trying to be nice. He had a crush on her; but bragging to be cool or jokingly scaring Sheri irritated her.

She sulked before giving in. "I'm sorry, what about him?"

Tim glimpsed a scruffy teen nail a half gainer off the low dive. "I wonder what's in his future."

"He's bound to be the next ghost host on 'Shock Theater.' He's an expert at giving people the creeps, especially me."

"Yeah—he's no Sean Connery."

"You see how he stares at me? He thinks there's something special between us."

"Is there?" Tim snickered.

"Don't be ridiculous. I'm nice to him the times we get together, but that's all. I hope he doesn't grow up to be a drooling pervert."

"Now you're being ridiculous."

"Maybe, but you don't watch him like I do: some of his expressions, especially his eyes; it doesn't take a rocket scientist to figure that he probably sees a . . . you know."

"A shrink?"

"Yeah, which reminds me . . . anyone can't help but wonder where his craziness comes from."

"From his mother or father?" Tim's temples fluttered.

Robert's parents seldom spoke to others. Tim and Sheri thought they were strict and overprotective. Robert's behavior surely had something to do with it. They enrolled him in a private school stressing that he mustn't take playtime seriously. Tim and Sheri often wondered what Mr. and Mrs. Bowden were like in private. Robert only mentioned that his father was in the carpet business and his mother was a *housemom*. When they'd attempt to probe deeper, he'd change the subject.

"Maybe it's not their fault." She shrugged. "Who knows why he turned out like, you know."

A vivid image sparked Tim's memory. "What about the stranger in the weird car; why hasn't Robert ever mentioned him?"

Occasionally Tim and Sheri noticed a stout middle-aged gentleman with slicked back hair and horn-rimmed glasses pull up to the Bowdens' driveway in a black Plymouth Valiant. Sporting an ivory colored button-down dress shirt, charcoal cardigan, and grey wool slacks, he'd enter the house, stay awhile, and escort Robert out—who knows where; but when they returned, Robert would always be licking an ice cream cone and smiling.

"Maybe he's a relative—no, wait, I know," Sheri perked up, "he's Robert's psychiatrist."

"So Robert *is* seeing a shrink and doesn't want us to know."

"Maybe, but I don't want to talk about it. Wait—look at the time! We'd better leave before Mom sends Mike or Dave."

Although he admired Sheri's brothers, the last thing Tim wanted was to have a teenager as a chaperone.

They snatched their towels and ran to the clubhouse. He knew she would shower before leaving. The front desk was empty, so Tim fiddled with some papers that lay there. Cold fingers darted up his spine. He jumped.

"Scared ya." Sheri grinned. "Come on, let's go."

"I'll race you home!" Tim shouted as their wheels spat gravel.

Tim wasn't sure what she'd had for breakfast, but she was beating him by a length. They settled in a patch of grass at the top of their street.

"I had a great time," her voice was bittersweet, "even if we did talk about Robert."

"Yeah," Tim sighed.

The wind kicked up and time faded. She stroked Tim's knuckles and giggled. To the shimmer of golden sunlight their shadows mingled in the lazy afternoon. She gently kissed his cheek. He soared—stars of joy whirled 'round him. Groping for the right words Tim gazed at the grass.

"Today was great. I'm glad you had fun."

"More than you'll ever know." She smiled dreamily.

The wind died, and with it came the inevitable:

"I wish I didn't have to leave," she frowned. "Guess I'll see you tomorrow."

"Yep," he nodded and watched her sail down the street, ebbing from sight, but never from his heart.

Beyond his bedroom window the halcyon glow from the tangerine horizon dissolved to velvet twilight. Tim nestled beneath the covers wishing his dreams would be as beautiful as their day.

Chapter 3

"Move it!" Tim shouted.

"Yeah!" Sheri shook her head. "We don't have all night!"

Like British redcoats they marched up the sidewalk through the crisp autumn air toting a flashlight and *The Ghostly Gallery*. A block away a lush willow tree adorned a neighbor's backyard like a mound of peacock feathers. It was the perfect place to tell scary stories. By daylight the willow's branches shielded them from tattletales who might notice they were on someone else's property. During the night, however, they had to be careful; someone might easily spot the glow from the flashlight they were using to read with. Tonight the Alfred Hitchcock book would have to wait. Robert had an incredible nightmare, an unbelievable experience: one they'd never forget. As they approached the willow, that second Friday in October of '67, they reminisced about being tricked and scared:

"Oh yeah?" Tim kicked the air. "It's happened to me plenty of times."

"Like?" Sheri twirled her hair.

"Like the time I was on the spook-house ride and the ticket taker decided to sneak in and tap me from behind. I screamed and smacked the friend sitting next to me so hard in the gut he almost threw up."

"Yeah," Sheri nodded, "that reminds me of the time I saw *The Tingler* on 'Shock Theater.'"

"Great movie!" Tim winked. "The one where Vincent Price—"

"Right—the one where the lobster crawls on everyone in the movie theater."

"Looked like a scorpion to me."

"Whatever," she shrugged. "Anyway, I was really into the movie. Just when the doctor's wife sicced the tingler on him, one of my brothers shook me. I shot up and slugged him like Muhammad Ali. He said that that was the last time he'd ever wake me to see 'The Late Show.'"

"How 'bout you?" Tim nudged Robert.

Robert loved monster movies and horror stories. He craved fantasy and escape. Tim and Sheri imagined him at bedtime closing the lid to his coffin, preparing for a savory night of blood sucking dreams.

"Look at him," she shook her head. "He's out to lunch again."

"Yeah—hey Robert!" Tim flicked his fingers. "Tell us your dream."

Few things thrilled Robert as much as recounting a hair-raising tale. Tim and Sheri marveled at his macabre stories. The moment he started they were spellbound. There was magic in his voice. He made them feel that they were his only friends. At night, in the dark, his voice was perfect: irresistibly smooth, yet delightfully eerie.

Imitating a mummy escaping from an ancient sarcophagus, he dragged his right foot; his hands were crossed over his chest.

"Snap out of it!" Tim barked.

Mystic poetry oozed from Robert's lips:

"The fateful bridge whispers to the sly moon, 'Should he reach the other side, there will be no doom.' Haunted by a gallop—it grows loud and louder—look up! Escape the fatal phantom on his manic steed; his fiery orb cocked, upon his boot a pumpkin seed. Shrouded in midnight gloom—always seeking, always feeding—the ghoul of Sleepy Hollow hounds me to an empty tomb."

"There he goes," Sheri sighed nervously.

Robert hadn't even started his story, and they were tingling with goose bumps.

"Wake up!" Tim clapped. "Say something."

Robert grinned at the sky and chanted his usual reply. "Nothing, nothing's wrong, you see; and what could be wrong? Nothing, nothing with me."

Tim noticed Robert returning to normal. "You're back!" Tim beamed.

Robert shook himself. "What do you mean?"

Sheri rolled her eyes.

"Never mind." Tim shrugged. "What about the dream?"

"I could really go for a scoop of vanilla ice cream."

"Chocolate's much better." Sheri crinkled her nose.

"I agree with Sheri, Robert; vanilla's a boring flavor."

"No way, you can do anything with it, put any type of syrup on it, or eat it plain and get off on the sweet, creamy flavor as it slides down your throat."

Sheri looked anything but amused, but before she could reply, Robert perked up.

"You'll never believe it—talk about a wild dream!"

Tim snickered, "Is it like the story where the gorilla goes ape?"

"Yeah," Sheri's eyes twinkled, "tell us about the gorilla again."

With a perverse grin he glared at them, then scratched and oohed like a baboon. "Nah, this dream's much better—trust me."

Dusk settled as they crept beneath the willows. Nestled with his friends Tim felt like he had come in from a frosty night and was kneeling beside a blazing fire. He was in seventh heaven. Sheri planned to read "Jimmy Takes Vanishing Lessons," but they were too excited to consider anything except Robert's dream . . . little did they know it would take up the entire evening. A thick patch of clouds blotted out the moon. It was so dark that they had to touch each other to confirm they existed. Sheri tossed the book on the fluffy grass. The wind nuzzled the willows. Probing his pockets for a Life Saver, the clatter from Tim's marbles prompted Sheri.

"Come on! I don't want anyone to catch us."

"Right," Tim nodded and whispered to Robert. "Remember reading the obituaries? We picked a name and called the funeral home. What did we say?"

Robert turned to Sheri, and with a haunting voice pretended to be the dearly departed speaking to the funeral parlor. "Hello Serenity Funeral Home? This is Jonathan Jones. I'd like to thank you for doing a nice job on my body." He clasped his throat pretending to choke himself.

"That's sick!" Sheri slapped his leg.

Robert continued. His face must have been turning blue.

"If you don't stop I'm leaving." She started to stand up.

"All right." He chuckled.

The next minute passed in silence, not counting the crickets chirping or the silky breeze that ruffled their hair. Flipping on his flashlight Robert leaned it against the tree trunk so that they'd have enough light to glimpse their outlines.

"Ready?" His whisper slit the night.

Tim and Sheri joined hands and nodded.

"I was in a cold sweat after it happened. Sheri, your family! I was floored."

"What about my family?" She quivered.

"Well . . ." He glared at her as if she were a long-lost ghost. "During the beginning of the dream, I was in my room reading my favorite paperback, *Vulture's Stew*. The dish of half melted vanilla ice cream was sheer delight. The clock on the dresser said seven. Mother and Father were gone. I was going to your home, Sheri. You and your brothers were playing board games. You must have invited me. I grabbed my penlight, a couple pieces of gum, and my good-luck charm: you remember John, the shrunken head I won at the carnival. I love rubbing his bony face and stroking his jet-black hair.

"The air was crisp, and the half-moon provided just enough light. A steady breeze rode my back as leaves twirled along the sidewalk. Each streetlight gleamed faintly. My mind called to sinister shadows that dared me to trek deeper into the restless night . . .

"On the steps of his Romanian castle, surrounded by cobwebs and dense fog, he appeared. His velvet cape rippled as he gestured for me to come closer. I cringed at his twisted face and pale skin. 'Fresh blood—who will give me blood? Will you?' He grinned. Fiery eyes pierced my brain; white fangs parted his ruby lips; stale breath seared my checks as he gorged on my neck. When I shook my head he disappeared.

"The Riddicks' house loomed in the moonlight. A slight chill trickled through me as I wondered why the lights were out. They can't all be asleep! I glanced at the chimney half expecting puffs of smoke, but nothing. Marching to the front door I pressed the buzzer twice—no answer. Nervously I tried the doorknob— it wouldn't budge. I swallowed the lump in my throat, darted around to the side, and tried the dining room—no luck. Anxious for a familiar face I raced to the cellar stairwell. Time tumbled to slow motion. I fell into a trance.

"'We're so happy you came,' whispered the sinister voices. 'It's time for you to feel the way we do, and then you'll know exactly what to do. But first you must find yourself . . . find yourself . . . fiiiiiinnnd!'

"I stumbled onto the landing. The voices stopped. As I peered into the cellar, the door sailed open—I was blind! That's how dark Mr. Riddick's workshop was. Surely the light switch . . . dead. I yanked out my penlight, and from the far wall appeared mounted hacksaws, drills, hammers, and chisels. There were gaps that indicated certain tools were missing. The jagged teeth of a circular saw glared, and from the machine a dark sludge patted the floor. I darted to the center of the basement. 'Sheri, Mike, Dave?' . . . nothing.

"To the left was a painting of a clipper ship, its hull torn against a jagged shore. Monster waves capsized the vessel. I detest waves. When I see them I picture hell, which is like drowning in a stormy sea.

"The painting hypnotized me. Then it devoured me. Drenched and shivering I kicked the frosty swirls. Miles from the ship, I knew I'd never reach shore. Fierce dragon swells hurled me into the deep: a fate of icy shadow and sea creatures gorging on me.

"Jolted by the painting, I spun around. A huge freezer chest pulsated in the distance. Like a deep-sea diver I lumbered to it.

Why couldn't I escape? I felt strapped in on a giant roller coaster
creeping up the first hill, the metal gears bumping and grinding,
forcing me to the top, rising so high I wondered whether I'd stand
the never-ending fall—as if someone threw me out of a jet at
20,000 feet! Something from the freezer called to me. I lifted the
lid and gagged: severed arms, legs, and torsos appeared. Blood
soaked ice crystals had formed on the remains. I pictured the
slime on the circular saw and realized its connection. Scrambling
upstairs I bolted to the front door, tripped, and blacked out."

Robert grinned at his playmates wondering how dearly they
were enjoying his dream. His Peter Lorre eyes were about to
explode. If anyone had jumped out to scare them, they would
have died of fright.

"That reminds me," Sheri cleared her throat. "Something
weird happened the other night."

Tim glanced at Robert curious whether he would object.

"Let's hear it." Robert cracked his knuckles and sighed,
annoyed that Sheri had dared to interrupt his show.

She glanced discreetly to the left and whispered. "Well . . .
last Saturday my family went to dinner and the movies. I would
have joined them, but I promised my friend, Pam, I'd help her
with her homework. I remember leaving after Mom cut my hair.
Anyway, we finished Pam's assignment in no time and tuned in
'The Carol Burnett Show.' They were doing a takeoff on *Sunset
Boulevard*. Carol was hilarious as Norma Desmond. Pam and I
were in stitches.

"I left after the show. Mom and Dad wouldn't be home yet, so I'd have a little time to myself. I was crossing Pam's backyard when she popped outside to join me. A full moon lit our way. As I glanced at the back of my home, my eyes twitched. The upstairs hall light was on. I nudged Pam and told her I was sure I had turned everything off before leaving. She thought my parents were home, but intuition hinted they weren't. A shadow darted from the hall into the bathroom, then vanished. We glanced at each other and blinked. I was frightened. Pam suggested we check to see if my father's car was in the driveway; if not, she'd convince her mom to let me stay until my family returned.

"The driveway was empty. Quietly we opened the front door and yelled, 'Anyone here?' No answer; nothing moved; the upstairs light was still shining. I slammed the door and we ran to Pam's. Half an hour later Mom phoned.

"When I told my brothers what had happened and asked if they noticed anything unusual when they came home, they shook their heads and shrugged. I wonder if there *was* a stranger in our house."

"Interesting." Robert seemed restless and surprised. "I had something like that happen to me once, but I—"

"Shh, quiet." Tim whispered.

The intruder scrambled through the dark—closer and closer. Sharp breaths and jingling pelted the air.

Clicking the flashlight off, Robert gasped, "Someone's coming to get us—I know it."

Tim raised a fist. "Sheri's not in the mood."

"They must have spotted the light!" she whispered frantically. "I knew we should've—who's that?" Sheri let out a muffled scream. "Oh, it's you," she sighed. "I almost peed in my pants."

"Who are you talking to?" Tim tried to cap his imagination.

"Yeah," Robert smirked, "what've you got?"

"Who else scampers on four paws and wears a leash? Quiet down Honey, it's okay," Sheri caressed the beagle.

"You said your brothers would take care of her." Tim groaned. "Now we'll never hear the rest of Robert's dream. Someone's bound to catch us."

"Honey's not whining and I haven't seen any neighbor's lights go on. Be quiet a minute."

They held their breath until Sheri whispered: "I think we're okay."

Tim slid beside her, grateful that Honey was on the opposite side.

"Thanks for not making a big deal about the dog." She clasped Tim's hand. The charms on her bracelet tickled his wrist. "I wish just the two of us were here."

Tim's heart rippled. He turned to Robert. "We're ready."

"I don't know," Robert mockingly replied, "maybe I'll finish another time."

This was a bluff. Robert thrived on attention. He just needed his ego oiled.

"Don't stop now!" they pleaded.

Robert smiled eerily as he clicked the flashlight on.

"Bolting from the bloody heap in the ice chest, I ran upstairs, tripped, and blacked out. When I came to, the gleam from my penlight illuminated Mr. and Mrs. Riddick's bedroom. As I gazed at the beautiful four-poster bed, visions of Ebenezer Scrooge shivering beneath the sheets flickered against the shadows. Then I saw Sheri's portrait. Her rag-doll image was hunched in an antique chair. It was hard to ignore her fish-like eyes. Gradually the canvas revealed itself: real flesh, eyes, hair, and lips were embedded in it. As I gaped she became super-charged, her body throbbing like an open heart. I dashed into the living room and slammed against a bookshelf. Stars exploded like Fourth-of-July fireworks. Sinking to my knees I drifted:

"The summer sun of the late afternoon nudged the mellow horizon as the noise from rides, barkers, and thrill seekers below blended into a soft, melodic hum. The motion of the Ferris wheel was so smooth that I grinned as the wheel lifted me high. Rounding the top Sheri appeared. She must have been telling a great joke because we roared with laughter. Gazing down, our mouths opened in awe as the streets began to shrink. The ride was growing in size. With each turn the wheel lifted us higher. Though the ride was expanding, the seats, as if they knew our wish was their command, remained the same size. A cool breeze made our eyes tingle—our hearts beat together— as we beamed shoulder to shoulder to the thrill of a lifetime. Higher and higher we jetted into the belly of an aqua sky. At the next turn we were so high that the Atlantic Ocean appeared—a gleaming sapphire carpet. Our cheeks glowed as we sailed like a child's blown bubbles through the dreamy air. Around again to the top brought us the entire Eastern United States Coast; yet for as high as we were, some incredible illusion let us glimpse the silvery miniature cars, houses, and stores that speckled the land. Through our smiles and laughter twilight arrived. In one brilliant surge, lights along the coast glittered like a million cat eyes. And looming above was a radiant moon whose mystic beams captivated our hearts. Holding hands, breathless to the wind, we gazed from the East Coast and sparkling Atlantic to foreign shores and the twinkling lights of England and Ireland; and to our restless ears echoed the faint clangs from Big Ben. 'Unbelievable!' we shouted. Up any higher and I was sure we'd soar into space. I squeezed Sheri; our lips moved closer; I closed my eyes and then she faded.

"'Don't leave me, please!' I snatched the air. For a moment she was a fragrant mist, and then, gone. I peered below and shuddered: the shores were black, the moon, grim, the ocean—hell. A thousand times I've imagined dying, but never like this, not to fall into that! I screamed as the Ferris wheel whirled 'round and 'round, faster it churned and then crashed, hurling me into the night. Swallowing a fist of air I fell in slow motion. The ocean was a bubbling valley of tar. I kicked and punched—I couldn't stop screaming. I was sure I'd be cremated, and then wham! I was in the Riddicks' living room panting and sweating.

"As I stood to catch my breath, moonlight flooded the room; and from the luminous space beyond, three heads appeared, each fixed to an adjoining window . . . the remains of Sheri's parents and her brother, Mike. Their eyeballs reeled in my direction. I ran to the kitchen desperate to protect myself—a knife, a cleaver, anything! Eyeing the counter I cringed. Inside the open breadbox lay Honey's body: her legs, drawn like a roped calf's; her eye sockets, empty. Next to the box were crystal salt-and-pepper shakers. Something was hideously wrong. I gasped. Honey's eyeballs were inside!"

Barely able to contain himself Robert paused—his eyes, wild; his grin, devious. Tim and Sheri wondered how much more they could take. Sheri stopped shivering and tensed. Something had clearly upset her. She let go of Tim's hand. Honey growled.

"What do you mean saying those things?"

"Huh?" Robert was dumbfounded.

"First it was my family: you mutilated them. Then, as if that wasn't enough, you stick Honey in the story. She's just an animal. She can't defend herself. Why did you kill her?—especially the part about Honey's eyeballs in the shakers. Why do you say those things?"

"Yeah!" Tim nodded. "You know Sheri hates cruelty to animals."

"Geez." Robert threw up his hands. "I can't control what happens in a dream; but I am sorry I upset you. I promise I won't mention Honey again."

He smiled at Sheri believing he would win her over. She completely ignored him.

"He didn't mean it," Tim whispered. "It was just a dream. Let him finish. Besides, I'm on your side. If he breaks his promise I'll pulverize him."

Tim caressed Sheri's arm. He could feel her starting to relax.

"I guess I'll forgive you." She shook her head at Robert. "But it's late. If I don't get home now, I'll be grounded forever."

"You can't leave!" He pleaded. "I'm getting to the best part—the end."

Tim nuzzled Sheri's cheek and whispered. "Please stay! A few extra minutes won't get you into any more trouble than you are in now. Besides, you know I like being with you. There's no one in the world that makes me feel this good."

"Hey!" Robert sounded jealous. "What are you whispering?"

She waved him off and blinked at Tim. "I'll stay, but only because you're here. I feel safe with you. You're my protector. I wish we could always be together."

Sheri nestled against Tim. Her soft curls warmed his cheek. As they held hands Tim felt like Captain America or the Green Lantern. He was invincible as long as she was by his side.

"I'll stay," she nodded.

"Great!" Robert rubbed his palms together and grinned.

As much as Tim and Sheri wanted to look away, they were transfixed. Tim couldn't help believing—he is a vampire! Breathlessly they waited for Robert's voice.

"I bolted from the kitchen to the front door. It wouldn't budge. Yet something unexpected gave me hope . . . a voice from upstairs. It sounded like Dave. I ran to him only to find that someone had left a radio on. The pale glow from the portable was all that illuminated Dave and Mike's room. If the radio was on, the electricity had to be. As I scrambled for a light switch, a skull-jarring blast rocked the house. Someone was trying to get in. I went into shock! The front door opened and lumbering feet pounded up the stairs. A thick shadow swallowed the hallway. I cried as I realized what would surely happen. The shadow drifted into the room and tripled in height. From the gleam of the radio, a surgical gown appeared; but this was no ordinary gown: it had been custom-made for a specific purpose. Tucked in its see-through pockets was a meat cleaver, a hacksaw, and an array of knives. I pictured the empty spaces on the wall in Mr. Riddick's workroom. The gown moved closer.

"My killer, he knows me, but do I know him? Something tells me I do. It's so familiar, the feeling I've been here, that this has happened before. I sense his every move and I know what comes next, but I won't face it—face, eyes, heart, soul, Devil! I know you, don't I?

"The gown was blood soaked. Lean fingers yanked out a steely dagger. He would make sure that by the time I reached the freezer, I was like the others—hacked and stacked. His eyes flared. It came to me but never finished: why did I feel so close to the stranger who would surely murder me?

"From the stale air his voice boomed. I thought it was my father—the bastard! But something about the tone put me so close to who it really was, I—.

"'Robert, it's me; don't you know me? I guess, as hard as you try, you'll never figure out who I am; but it won't matter because it'll all happen like it's supposed to. I've made frozen food out of your friends, and now I'm going to make you as sorry as that shrunken head in your pocket.' He screamed and charged.

"Jumping to the side, I slammed into the opposite wall. Before passing out, a burst of light revealed a haunting image. The killer lay face down, his arms positioned like a cliff diver's, his hands glued to the weapon that had barely missed me; it had pierced the light socket. The shock thoroughly electrocuted him.

"When I came to, smoke filled the air. His hands clutched the dagger still planted in the light socket. I raced downstairs; and as I hit the landing, my jacket snagged the closet doorknob. Something stiff popped out—lips smeared my cheek. I shoved it away. The mysterious shape bounced back like a sack of potatoes and propped itself upright in the closet. I cocked my penlight and screamed! The stale corpse of Dave Riddick appeared. I tore from the house into the night. I had to tell someone what happened. I woke up shivering. I kept reminding myself, 'It's just a dream.' I never did get back to sleep."

Robert's flashlight gleamed faintly, and the once playful breeze vanished. It was ten o'clock—Tim knew that no excuse would be good enough: better to be honest even if he did get swatted with the belt. As he released Sheri's hand she pounded the ground, glared at Robert, and shook her finger.

"You should have told us it was gonna be this long before you started. I'm really gonna get it. I always find a way to BS Mom and Dad, but they're never going to believe—"

"It won't do any good." Tim nudged her and pointed.

Robert was shell-shocked.

She shook her head and gazed at Tim. A faint smile parted her lips. "I have to leave, though I wish I could stay out all night. Snap him out of it and make sure he gets home. Who knows what his parents will do. Come on, Honey," she gently tugged the dog's collar. Honey shook herself and panted.

Tim nodded, "I'll take care of him. I'll talk to you tomorrow."

"I don't think we'll be seeing or talking to one another for a while."

"Try to."

"I'll do my best," she squeezed Tim's hand, kissed his cheek, and ran home. The jingle of Honey's tags faded to a faint tinkle.

Tim glowed as he mooned over Sheri. He pictured they were beside a roaring fire confiding their deepest secrets. Something behind him stirred.

"Where are we?" Robert burst thru the willows. "Where is Sheri?"

"I'll tell you in a minute. Grab the book and let's go."

Following Tim to the sidewalk Robert stared at Tim's watch. "I'm really in trouble!"

"So am I. Sheri left a few minutes ago. She's probably home."

"I was really into the dream. I should have only told half of it."

"That was some story. We were shakin' in our shoes. I've never heard anything half as crazy."

"I couldn't believe it myself. I had to tell someone." He rubbed his eyes.

"There is one question Sheri wanted me to ask."

Robert blinked and nodded.

"Who was the killer in the dream?"

Robert squinted. "I'm not sure. He seemed familiar. When I figure it out I'll tell you." Robert waved goodbye.

"Wait." Tim raised a hand. "You know the secret place you found a year ago and fixed up? I'd like to see it sometime. Where did you say it was?"

Tim and Sheri were more than curious about Robert's hideout; but every time they asked, Robert declined to show them. They often wondered whether it existed. Maybe it was one of the many figments of Robert's overactive imagination. Robert said that he stumbled onto it one windy afternoon when he was trying to lose himself. He looked around and there it was: a place with great potential. Robert spent hours making it decent. Eventually it became a second home. Inside he could say or do anything with no one giving him funny looks or trying to discipline him.

He turned to Tim, and for a moment Tim felt lucky; but Robert shook his head. "Not now. Besides, if I told you, it would no longer be my secret place."

Tim was ticked. "I thought I was your best friend. Come on; I promise I won't tell anyone, not even Sheri." That was a lie, but Tim was desperate.

"I need a place where I can be alone. I spent a lot of time fixing it up for that purpose. You are my best friend, believe me. Maybe in a year I'll show you—please understand."

The concern on Robert's face and his sincerity coaxed Tim to give in. He'd bug Robert later. "Okay, but there is one question you could answer."

"If I don't get home now—" Robert fidgeted.

"Just tell me who the stranger is who drops by."

"What?" Robert shrugged.

"You know, the guy with the horn-rimmed glasses who drives the weird black car. He takes you out for ice cream and—"

"I don't know what you're talking about, honestly."

"Never mind." Why pursue it Tim figured. If the guy really was Robert's shrink, Robert would be too embarrassed to discuss it.

As they parted, Tim gazed at the murky sky and shivered over Robert and his crazy quirks. Tim was on restriction for three weeks—what a pain.

For quite a while Tim and Sheri obsessed over Robert's nightmare: the one childhood tale that left an indelible impression.

Chapter 4

"Azoo!" Bish slammed his lunch tray down and dropped into his chair. "You know how I convinced my brother not to cream your ass? . . . by promising him you'd not only cover the cost of the upholstery job, but you'd give his Corvair a decent wash and wax job, which you will do 'cause I'll be there to supervise."

Gazing at his napkin Azoo buttered his bread. "All right, I won't argue . . . guess I have it coming."

"Sure as shit do." Naylor twirled his pasta.

The clamor of high school students gabbing and chowing was ideal for Bish and company's impromptu summit.

"My brother was decent enough to consider lending me his car again." Bish cracked open his milk. "Of course that was after I gave him the rest of the Waheekan Gold. You owe me, man."

"You didn't. Damn it!" Naylor kneed Azoo. "You always screw up a cherry situation. That weed was primo. What a waste; don't know when we'll cop another choice batch."

Azoo ate slowly, hoping the subject would shift.

"So bizarre stumbling on that severed head." Bish frowned. "I can't figure who in our neighborhood would do anything that twisted."

"Maybe a pervert or a New York mobster," Naylor shrugged.

Azoo licked his lips and cringed. "And the face on the head."

Naylor tapped Bish. "I still say it looked like Ed Sullivan underwater."

"It did look like a wigged out zombie." Bish bit off half of his garlic toast.

"What about the stitches around the mouth?" Naylor quivered.

Azoo cleared his throat. "Maybe the killer suffocated the guy by sewing his mouth shut."

"Dork." Naylor nudged him. "His nose would have also been stitched shut."

"The murderer could have taped it shut and then, once the guy was dead, ripped the tape off."

"You think too much." Bish glared. "Though if we knew what the inscription on the bag, R and J, stood for, it might reveal that the killers were a couple of our neighbors."

"I told you: R and J are for Runt and Jerkoff." Naylor pitched his thumb at Azoo.

"Kiss off, Naylor—snake."

Bish thumped the table. "Enough!"

Twisted half around one of Hammond cafeteria's pillars, two yards from Bish and his classmates, Tim was ringing with awe. The gossip was too tantalizing to ignore. As he whiffed the tempting aroma of spaghetti, he pressed his cheek against the pale green ceramic tiles and kept listening.

"Naylor, are you sure you didn't stash the head in your parent's cellar?" Bish wolfed down a wad of pasta, chasing it with a chug of milk. "You were drooling over it like it was a winning game ball."

"No freaking way," Naylor snorted. "I may have thought it was a cool, maybe kidded you that I wanted it; but I'm smart enough to avoid major jail time. Though I did get carried away—must have been the buzz from that kickass weed. Besides," Naylor nodded at Azoo, "he was the first one to check the creek Sunday morning."

Azoo's fork tumbled into his salad. "I told you before that I have no idea who copped it. All I know is that yesterday, when I went there, the head and bag were gone."

"Come on Naylor, confess." Bish winked as he probed Naylor's eyes.

"Fuck you; fuck both of you!" Naylor kicked his chair back and slapped his milk carton down; a spurt squirted across the table, inches from Bish's shirt. "If I look at you like I'm doing, and tell you right out that I didn't touch the freaking head, you'd damn well better believe me," he glared, "or our friendship—"

"Cool down." Bish nodded at the table of sophomores who seemed to be hanging on Bish's reply. "I believe you; guess I had to be sure."

Keeping his eyes locked on Bish, Naylor eased his chair back to the table.

Bish leaned forward and spoke softly. "I just can't figure where in the hell it vanished to. I don't think Azoo took it. Why would he and then lead us back the next morning and show us it was missing?"

"What about it, Azoo?" Naylor clenched his fists.

"Bullshit. Don't pin this on me. I told you to call the police two nights ago when we found it. Hell, I'll call them now and tell them, though I doubt it would do any good."

"Fuck if you will." Bish yanked Azoo's collar while straining to speak softly. "All we need is for our asses to get roasted by being accused of shit we didn't do, if or when they find the head. If you value yours you'll shut up."

Naylor shrugged. "I don't see any harm telling friends: you know, like" he smiled at Jan, "your girl."

"Maybe." Bish let go of Azoo's shirt and poked his steady. "Hey babe, what's shakin'? Take a seat." He turned to Naylor. "There's nothing there so who'd believe us? But no cops: telling them would be like selling them pot—perpetual harassment."

"Right!" Naylor and Azoo clacked their fists in agreement.

The second time their fists hit, Bish joined them. "All for none or none at all!" they chanted and chuckled.

"What are you all revved about? What's with the cops and selling them pot?" Jan nudged Bish as she hopped beside him and wound her leg around his.

"Carol, Tim Carol!"

"Wha—" Tim's gut flickered. Dave Riddick's leer was always humbling, especially when he caught Tim off guard.

"Where's my English composition?"

"Right." Tim whipped the front of his shirt up, yanked out the assignment, and handed it to Sheri's brother.

"What's this, Carol, sweat on my homework? Lucky for you it's only on the back of the last page."

"I was in a hurry. I have to get back before recess ends."

"Just kidding," Dave grinned. "Thanks for running it up from Polk School. So Sheri told you where I usually sit?"

Tim nodded. Dave's impish smirk could win anyone over. His sincere blood-brotherly glow eclipsed his sarcasm. Add Dave's natural good looks to the mix, and it was obvious why Tim often longed to be Dave.

"I was pissed at myself when Mrs. Dix from the front office told me that Mom called about me forgetting my paper; but then she said that Mom mentioned you'd be dropping it off. Relief! God knows my older brother's too busy to run home; Sheri is always doing me favors; and me: I do appreciate having the time to digest a decent lunch."

"Mmm." The sexy brunette winked at Dave as she brushed seductively against his shoulder. "Where's Allison?"

"Some important business, helping her mom. She'll be back for 4th period."

"Well if you're lonesome when your friend leaves," she flashed a bewitching smile at Tim, "don't hesitate to keep me company."

"I hear you." Dave grinned as she twitched her hips and sensuously strolled to her table.

"Sweet babe—what's her name?" Tim sighed goo-goo eyed.

"Carol, stop drooling. She's not your type; besides, you're too old for her?"

"Man, I wish!" Tim kept imagining.

"Earth to Tim," Dave snapped his fingers. "So I guess Sheri or Mom talked you into bringing my paper."

Tim shook himself from fantasy. "When your mom mentioned it to Sheri this morning, as we were leaving for school, I thought I'd lend a hand."

"Nice, buddy; now I'm sure—when Miss Kritch collects the assignments—not to ruffle her southern hospitality. I—"

"Ah ha," Bish kneed the table and grinned, "I do believe one of the Riddick boys is rapping with a grade-schooler. I had a sneaking suspicion you were square; now there's no denying it."

"Excuse me, Tim." Dave pitched a hand through his sleek auburn hair before firing his blues on Bish. "I guess it's time for 6th graders to get back to class."

Tim turned to leave, but his feet were locked: the anticipation of Dave's reaction was riveting.

"Yeah, Bish?" Dave leaned back. "I'm surprised you and your Jell-O headed buddies escaped from elementary school. You must have paid beaucoup bucks for copies to all the exams."

"Fuck off!" Naylor pointed.

"Right!" Azoo stomped.

"Easy Dave." Jan frowned.

"Riddick?" Bish hopped up and flexed his shoulders. "It seems, every time we talk, sooner or later I get your dickwad remarks . . . only today they seem to be sputtering from your ass instead of your mouth."

"Maintain, Bish." Jan hissed to deaf ears and squeezed his arm.

"You ought to know," Dave eased from his seat and moved face to face with Bish. "You've been sitting on your brain since you were a freshman; only the Kentucky-fried weenies you hang with fail to see the obvious."

Naylor and Azoo jumped beside Bish. A third of the students were up, itching for a fight; some goaded for blood; some shouted for it to stop.

"That remark was just what I needed to shred your nuts." Bish shoved Dave and cocked his fists.

Riddick leaned in to return the push when a roar rocked the cafeteria. Tim whirled and blinked.

"Gentlemen! . . . and ladies."

The tide of seething teens froze. There was no doubt as to the intruder's identity. Though he was often amicable, Mr. Boyd's grimace could render any hostile student impotent. Tim peered at Bish who recoiled and grunted. The assistant principle rubbed his steely palms together as he sauntered toward the crowd.

"This can't be a pep rally. We don't play T. C. Williams for another two weeks."

Students—some frustrated, some relieved—returned quietly to their lunch.

"I strongly suggest for those of you still standing," Boyd squinted with disappointment at Dave, pivoted, and glared at Bish, "to take your seat and continue lunch. Or for those who find my office irresistible . . ." With a telltale smile he pinched his lips. "I will accommodate." Boyd nodded to a subdued crowd. "Now I believe everyone can resume dining and socializing." He briskly turned and strutted from sight.

Tim waved farewell to Dave as he scrambled from the cafeteria down Pegram Street, racking his head for the right excuse for wandering from the playground.

The teens' account of the severed head smoldered in Tim's mind until Sheri mentioned it. The incident had quickly circulated around Hammond; Dave informed her.

"Yeah," her nose crinkled, "coming from those jugheads—my brother's often scoffed at how flaky they are—it has to be nonsense, kind of like one of Robert's tales, minus the plot."

Robert nodded when Tim told him. "Sounds pretty cool; reminds me of a scene from a science fiction chiller: you know, like *The Brain That Wouldn't Die*."

Chapter 5

On the night flight to his D. C. appraisal seminar, the jet engines purred while the faint hiss from the overhead air nodules reminded Tim of a child letting the air out of a tire. He glanced at the passengers spread thinly throughout the cabin. Some napped while others read, worked crossword puzzles, or smiled to tunes; yet he couldn't help imagining them grinding their hearts out at their day jobs: tight faces with pursed lips and intense eyes—so cold, calculating, analytical, quick to judge, *never* satisfied—desperate for approval and to get ahead, to make it in the fast-food dysfunctional world they thrived on where the only relief from nerve-racking stress, which fueled ulcers, migraines, breakdowns, and quitting your job, was food, sex, booze, drugs, the internet, video, and TV. Here it was, ten months into the new millennium, so long awaited—an age where everyone dreamed of building a brighter future—yet the idea of the perfect job or a relaxed life seemed as unlikely and imaginary as time travel. As hard as it was to swallow, Tim realized that over the years, he, to some extent, had become one of them. Shrugging off his disgust he nursed his double' Hennessy on ice and recalled: not so long ago meals were better and flight bottles of liquor, complimentary—along with more leg and elbow room. Tim's thoughts drifted to scenes from *The Best Years of Our Lives*. Stoked by the characters and setting, he wondered what had become of America, her simplicity, and sincerity: the U.S. had been transformed and streamlined into neurotic mindsets and 24/7 dismal news. The stars from '*Best Years*'—Dana Andrews, Teresa Wright, Fredric March, Myrna Loy, Harold Russell, and Hoagy Carmichael—they'd be at Butch's Place . . . Tim imagined talking, drinking, laughing, and dancing the night away with them.

Though he had finished rummaging through his childhood, the story was far from over. Certain recent incidents made him wonder—others made him worry.

Months after Robert's infamous nightmare Tim and his family moved to Seattle. During high school he lost touch with Sheri; last he'd heard, she'd moved and so had Robert, but to where? He was clueless. Days, seasons, and years passed—his transformation, like fertile earth to a vibrant orchard. His playmates from Northern Virginia were distant memories until a year before his flight: Tim was in Pittsburgh visiting his cousin, lounging in her living room late Saturday morning.

"What's up?" She playfully nudged him.

Short and slender with Grecian skin, buoyant eyes, and dark locks, Cathy teamed with energy.

"Thought I'd browse." He waved an old *white pages*.

"There's plenty we can do. I was checking the paper and—"

"That's okay; think I'll relax and—" Suddenly, from the B's popped Robert C. Bowden. "Hmm."

"What?" She motioned as if she were hailing a taxi.

"The weird playmate from my old neighborhood: you remember Robert Bowden. He used to hang with the Riddicks and me—quiet, dark hair, large eyes."

"You probably mentioned him, though I don't remember meeting him."

Tim stared at the listing. "Screwball kid, but man could he tell a story. Think I'll try this number."

"Whatever." Cathy shrugged. "How 'bout lunch? I have burgers and fries, or how 'bout a salad?"

"You know what I think of rabbit food."

Tim's pulse soared as he contemplated calling. Finally he snatched the receiver . . . ten rings and no answer. The aroma from the sizzling beef drifted in from the kitchen.

Cathy lives in an agreeable suburb of hardworking middle-class who for the most part keep tabs on each other. Built on an overlook of mature trees and rich green grass, the neighborhood is bounded by miles of storefronts, restaurants, and a few malls, all situated below on McKnight and Babcock roads. North Hills is relatively quiet except on occasional summer evenings when a musical serenade from an accordion band at the nearby Croatian center spells the night with waltzes and polkas. There's a land-mark a few minutes from Cathy's at the corner of People's Plank and Babcock roads, a life-size wooden bear standing on its hind paws. Every time Tim glimpses it he realizes he's seconds from his cousin's hospitality.

Tim tried again after lunch, but no luck. He jotted down the address. Cathy confirmed it on a map and advised him of the quickest route.

"Want me to come?"

"Best that I go alone." He slipped into his shoes.

"That'll give me time to run some errands and get grocer-ies; but be careful. You said that the guy's weird. I don't want my favorite cousin ending up in the obituaries."

"Robert? We've always seen eye to eye. See ya soon."

Tim departed smooth and sure in his new convertible. He had enjoyed driving it so much, he figured this time, instead of flying from Seattle to see Cathy, he'd tour the country while breaking in his new toy. Although the trip to his cousin's had been pleasant, and Tim was enjoying his stay, it was time to indulge in something he hadn't pondered in ages. It'd be cool to reminisce with Robert and catch up on lost years, if the address was right. The listing was in Shadyside, 20 minutes away.

He coasted down Greenhill Road, steep and wooded, turned onto Babcock Boulevard and followed it through the town of Millvale. Eyeing the familiar storefronts and row houses, Tim realized why many motion picture studios used Pittsburgh as a backdrop for their movies: so many unique locations in one metropolis. Bits of Millvale, brooding and dismal, sparked Tim to envision he was on the set of an old-fashioned main street in a black-and-white Jimmy Cagney movie with machine guns rattling and bombs exploding plate-glass windows.

Snagging Route 28 Tim headed downtown. As he barreled over the 40th Street/Washington Crossing Bridge, he smiled at the cast-iron emblems, replicas of the state seals from the original 13 colonies. It was here—on a fateful December night, before the last French and Indian War—that George Washington and his guide, Christopher Gist, were returning from a conference with the French. While attempting to traverse the Allegheny, Washington stumbled from his raft into the frigid water and nearly drowned . . . Neither George nor Mr. Gist uttered a word as Tim crossed the bridge, at least none that he could sense.

Tim followed 40th Street to Liberty Avenue, just south of Allegheny Cemetery. Famous nineteenth-century celebrities including songwriter Stephen Foster and singer/actress Lillian Russell would no doubt be among the countless ghosts wandering the grounds. Through Lawrenceville and Bloomfield Tim rambled, then into Shadyside—this was where he hoped to find Robert. Noting the addresses on College Street, Tim pulled over and flinched. Intuition hinted that Robert dwelled in the house that commandeered Tim's gaze.

The dark Victorian loomed like a dungeon in a wheat field: built circa 1880, its charred chimneys, slate shingles, and massive turret made Tim marvel at what internal treasures he might discover. The wraparound oak porch and half-moon shaped, leaded-glass windows evoked images of a simpler time; however, something about the house made Tim cringe—memories of how Robert used to glare like Count Dracula. This house fit Robert perfectly . . . Tim traipsed onto the creaky porch, the door slowly opened, and a grim face shattered the dark. He gasped! It was Robert peering with sinister eyes and a dismal smile, beckoning Tim inside . . . A sigh of relief cooled the sweat on Tim's brow. Exiting from his daydream he recognized the house number—he was at the wrong address.

Tim continued cruising down College. The neighboring homes, built in the 1920s, were smaller. When it appeared, it was quite different from the Victorian. Though the sun was drawn to portions of it, the house was eerie in its own way: a brooding, chocolate-colored three-level Colonial with a jutting front parlor and an enormous pyramid dormer. Tim parked opposite the driveway. The glimmer from the stately brass numerals above the front door roused his curiosity. He snatched his mini binoculars, a handy tool of the seasoned real estate appraiser. A bright pulsating blob flooded the lenses. He tuned in and realized the elegant curves of a heart shaped doorknocker. From the way it glistened Tim swore it was silver or silver-plated. Words forged across its center read:

FATAL DREAMS

The engraving was stylish, yet somehow the more he peered at it the more restless he felt: some morbid future revelation, but what? He tossed the binoculars onto the passenger seat and hopped out. The house and driveway looked vacant. He was scanning the windows, sipping the crisp autumn air, when a stranger who Tim later learned was in his late seventies approached and introduced himself. Dressed in worn checkered slacks, a pale dress shirt, a yellow Members Only jacket, and mail-order shoes, the slightly unshaven skin-and-bones geezer had a long haggard face and granny glasses, all of which made him look like he was pushing ninety. He told Tim that he lived a block away. Tim mentioned Robert and his old neighborhood in Virginia, then asked if he had the right guy. John nodded, shuddered slightly, and whined:

"Robert? They took care of him, all right—put him away for good. He's in the local nut house. It all happened a few years ago. Guess ya didn't hear . . . he murdered his parents."

Tim's stomach churned . . . Killed his parents? Could he really have done something that hideous? Tim scanned the silver-haired codger with doubt, wondering what he'd say next.

"The papers said that Robert somehow got the crazy notion his folks and closest friends were out to get him. He swore up and down he was gonna see 'em all die first. One of these days, when he feels like it, he'll march out of that place." John shook his finger at Tim.

"How?"

"A couple of his friends work there. My son, Timmy, used to hang with Robert and his buddies. Timmy told me what a whiz Robert was with computers. He said that Robert could get information on anyone or anything he wanted, it didn't matter how impossible it seemed. But I guess he won't be doing that for a while."

"Where's he at?"

"You're not really gonna go there and see him, are you?"

John gripped his chest as if he'd just run a marathon, and then it hit. Tim backed up three paces to clear the air. The stench from the mammoth flutterblaster lingered in the air like rotten salami. Tim was surprised the mere force didn't blow out the seat of the old-timer's pants. He kept jabbering as if nothing had happened.

"Whoa!" Tim fanned himself trying his hardest not to give John hell.

"Somethin' wrong?" A faint smile crinkled his lips.

"Not at all," Tim grimaced. "Everything is roses."

"What'd ya say?"

"Never mind—just tell me where he is."

Tim yanked out a notepad and jotted down the address of the facility.

"You can visit all you want, but it ain't gonna do you a lick of good."

"Why?" Tim rolled his eyes.

Leaning to the side, John forked his fingers under his nose: the old farmer's handkerchief. He blew three times and snot went flying. Passing gas was one thing, but this was the limit. Tim shook his head as John wiped his slimy hands on the front of his slacks. Tim couldn't look at him.

"Why?" Tim asked again.

"Why what?"

"You were saying that it wouldn't do me a lick of good."

"Oh, right. What I meant was that you can go down and talk to the people there, but they ain't gonna let ya see him."

"Because?"

"He's in a medium-security ward."

"Medium-security?" Tim winced. "Why the hell isn't he in maximum-security?"

"The place doesn't have it."

Tim thought: this guy ought to know—he belongs there.

"My boy—that's Timmy, you know—told me they had Robert in a maximum-security hospital, but after a while they sent him to the place he's at now for more tests and evaluations."

"Why can't I see him?"

"You'd have to be a blood relative, or one of them state shrinks, or a guard who works there, or you'd have to get clearance and that doesn't come overnight."

Tim raised his hand. "I hear you."

John was right. If Tim really wanted to see Robert, he'd have to think of a grand-slam plan. Maybe Cathy could help.

Tim waved goodbye and dashed to his convertible. With a wily smirk he squealed from the curb and flipped John the bird. In his rear view the feisty coot trampled the sidewalk, flailed his fists, and cursed the sky. Tim rolled with laughter as he raced to his cousin's. All the way back he thought of nothing but Robert. Tim had to see him. Maybe just by looking at him, he could figure out whom, over the years, he had become, and what had driven him to murder his parents.

Twenty minutes later Tim was at Cathy's. She had left the front door unlocked. As he exited the bathroom the familiar click of her shoes against the flagstone walk echoed. He was at the threshold to greet her.

"Excuse me, lady," Tim snickered, "but whatever you're selling we don't want it."

"Then I guess these delicacies will go to waste." She winked.

"Food! That's different. Come in and make yourself at home. The woman who owns the place will be back any minute."

"Ha," Cathy snapped her fingers, "she's right here."

Tim helped store the groceries, then plunked down on the living room sofa.

"So what happened? What did you find?" She settled beside him.

"Something you wouldn't believe."

"Like?"

"Robert did something I never would have expected." Tim cleared his throat and swallowed. "He murdered his parents."

"What?" Cathy's eyes flared. "How?"

"I didn't think to ask the grubby geezer who updated me on Robert, but I did find out where they're holding him." As Tim relayed the specifics her voice perked up.

"That's a coincidence. About a week ago my best friend, Fran, gave me a pamphlet on the place: a history of Pittsburgh's treatment of the poor and insane over the last 200 years including a rundown on that state hospital. Her husband, Ed—super-nice guy—works as a guard for the deranged convicts."

"Really." Tim's heart revved. Here was his chance. "I need a favor, big time. You may think I'm crazy, but for personal reasons I'd like to see Robert. If you could get Fran to talk to Ed, maybe he could figure a way to get me in and—"

"You're kidding? First you tell me how weird Robert is, then you race across town hunting him down, and now, after you discover he murdered his parents, you still wanna see him? I don't get it."

"Robert was strange and no doubt he murdered his parents, but I knew him long before he stripped his gears. When we were kids I was probably his only true friend. I took him seriously and admired him for his extraordinary imagination. He must have snapped after I moved to Seattle. I feel partially responsible for how he turned out. I just want to see his face. I don't need to talk to him. I know it sounds strange, but I'd feel better."

Cathy had never denied Tim a favor, yet this one seemed senseless. Though Tim's logic bewildered Cathy, her loyalty to blood was impeccable.

"I *have* done my share of favors for Fran and Ed, like the time I gave them Steelers' tickets to four home games. You could say they owe me one good turn."

Tim tapped her lightly on the knee. "Do this and I'll treat to dinner at one of your favorite restaurants. We'll start with a bottle of choice wine and a few hors d'oeuvres, then the main course—fresh lobster and a thick porterhouse steak; afterwards, a delectable dessert plus a few cordials: how's that sound?"

"You don't have to wine and dine me. You know I do you favors when I can. Of course if you want to pay for dinner, I won't object, and right now that sounds great; but I can't predict what Fran's husband will say about sneaking you in. Ed could lose his job; and I value their friendship too much to forfeit it over a favor."

"As long as you try, I'll understand if Ed says 'no'; dinner's still on me. All I ask is that you give it your best shot—please."

She meditated for a moment . . . "You win. I'll call Fran, and if she's home—"

"Beautiful!"

"I hear ya, but wait." Cathy raced upstairs, darted back, and thrust what looked like a high-school term paper into Tim's hands. "Check this out." She headed to the kitchen.

"When you talk to Fran, don't forget to tell her to ask Ed if Robert Bowden is at the hospital."

Tim curled up on the couch, engrossed in the history of Pittsburgh's poor and insane. He was reading the part about the facility where Robert was staying when Cathy popped into the living room.

"I talked to Fran and she's willing to give it a go. Ed's there today. She'll call him and see what he thinks. If Robert is there, assuming Ed approves, you may be driving down in a few hours. She'll call me as soon as she knows."

Tim pitched her a thumbs up and continued reading. It was 2:15 when the phone rang. He dropped the pamphlet. "Come on!" a voice inside him screamed.

She rushed to him waving her hands like an irate Italian. "Hey, what's the matter, you!" she roared and smiled. "So when are we dining?"

He shook his fists. "How'd you do it?"

"Charm, I guess, but look: Fran told me Ed wants you to leave in 15 minutes. He goes on break in an hour. It'll take 45 minutes to get there. That gives me time to give you the specifics on Ed and where he'll be, plus give you directions. Please be careful."

"I'll be a diplomat."

"That's not what I meant."

"Sure, and Robert?"

"He's there."

Chapter 6

The highway parted the rock-treed hills smooth and sure like a diamondback rattler slithering through a quarry. Small factories and stretches of town flickered as sunlight danced across the windshield. Tim exited onto a sleepy two-lane road with a few rustic shops and a convenience store, then to woods. From the mid-afternoon shadows the faded blue sign to the sanitarium seemed to nod nonchalantly. He veered onto a winding lane flanked by trees whose branches strained to smother his windshield—perhaps they would strangle his car. Cruising along a steep ridge Tim's eyes flickered as it reared from the opposite end of the valley: the dated jumble of brick and stone that jolted the air like a gothic castle. Tim was startled . . . as if a centipede had crawled up his leg, or a whirlwind had touched down, or the eyes of a stranger had unexpectedly blinked from behind the closet hangers. Focusing on the valley he began to unwind. Soft, silvery peaks surrounded it. A quiet stream rippled through the center where beautiful fields glistened. He wondered what tell-tale secrets he might discover during his visit. As his car whistled downward, a soul quenching breeze swished his face.

At the floor of the valley, the main road was aged, white-washed macadam; not a white or yellow line divided it. Maintaining its posted speed of 30, Tim's convertible glided through the grounds. He blinked at the yawning weathered gates. Concrete benches with thick wooden slats nestled on the kelly-green grass. He had arrived.

The State hospital is a medium-security corrections facility and asylum for the mentally ill. Inmates are assigned there from jails, prisons, and psychiatric hospitals. Dangerous criminals are confined to the Forensic Center for 30 to 90 days, long enough to determine whether they are mentally fit to stand trial. Those judged competent and guilty are sent to prison; the insane ones depart to other asylums for long-term care.

Tim daydreamed to the hospital structures: century old and run-down plus a few from the 1940s, and one mid-'60s admissions center; the half that appeared vacant were ready for the wrecking ball. The older architecture reminded Tim of bleak monasteries, which transformed into mud-caked swamp creatures wheezing to the autumn sky. In their youth, as brutal dungeons, they gorged on generations of misfits; but like the inevitable change in Dorian Gray's portrait, they were now crippled with rot and decay.

From the report Cathy had handed him, Tim envisioned ghostly inmates from the institution's past, including the paupers and the retarded who in the early days were placed with the insane and the criminals because no other place would care for them. Dressed in dark-blue denim (their hair in short bangs) their grim expressions riddled Tim with apprehension and pity. He imagined their snake-pit existence: the iron fences; barred windows; overcrowding; inadequate staff; screams at night; stink of sweat, vomit, and bedpans; years of grueling labor in the nearby coal mines; prescribed treatments of alcohol, morphine, Benzedrine, and convulsion-inducing Metrazol; scalding and freezing high-pressure hoses; muzzles and straitjackets; electro and insulin shock; and lobotomies. The report mentioned rapes and murders committed in the nearby suburbs 10 to 20 years ago by a few of the hospital's fugitives. Tim hesitated to think what Robert would do if given the chance.

In the small lot across from the Forensic Center there was a dozen cars including a county police and sheriff's cruiser. From a narrow strip of grass hailed a chalk-white sign with bold letters:

**PARKING ON THE HOSPITAL GROUNDS
IS AT YOUR OWN RISK.
OFFICIAL STATE BUSINESS ONLY.
NO TRESPASSING.
USERS OF PARKING AREA
MUST ASSUME LIABILITY
FOR THEIR OWN VEHICLES AND CONTENTS.**

Tim spotted Fran's Camry and rolled beside it. Ed's Jeep was in the shop, and so he had borrowed his wife's car. He was perched behind the wheel singing to Lynyrd Skynyrd's *Gimme Three Steps*. Ed had the windows down; a double-corona Macanudo smoldered in the ashtray. He grinned mischievously as he grooved to the beat. His husky voice was on key and sounded good. His massive hands battered the dashboard as he belted out the lyrics. He nodded at Tim. Tim waved, trying his best not to bust out laughing, introduced himself, then hopped into the Camry.

"Nice to meet you." Ed punched the volume down, popped the cigar to his lips, and cocked his head to blow a stream of smoke out the window.

"Likewise—I love cigars." Tim whipped out an Ashton Cabinet, wet the butt, and peeled away the tip before asking Ed if he minded.

"Hell no, that's a primo smoke." Ed winked as Tim fired up his cigar.

"Here," Tim nodded, exhaled, and pulled another Ashton from his jacket.

"You don't have to give me that."

"It's the least I can do."

"I'm sure Cathy mentioned the Steelers' tickets she slipped Fran at no charge, plus the other favors. Sure you don't want this back?"

Tim shook his head.

"Much obliged." He tucked it in the glove compartment and smiled—a nice smile. "I'll have that tonight after dinner."

"Sounds good. Oh, what about parking? The sign says—"

"You won't be here long enough." A halo of smoke sailed from his lips.

Ed was in his mid-forties, hefty from beer and good eating, but strong as a bull. His mocha-brown hair, turquoise eyes, pear-shaped clean-shaven face, and infectious grin pegged him for 15 years younger. He was laid-back, but jovial—the kind of guy you'd have a blast with whether you were hitting the bars and clubs, or kicking back watching a movie.

"Cathy tells me you're a commercial appraiser. What's that like?" He took a swig of Coke.

"Tedious."

"Tell me about it. Say, I wonder what the value of this heap is?" He pointed to a few of the buildings.

"After surveying the site, interviewing management here and at comparable facilities, examining income/expense statements, plats, and records at the courthouse, plus checking the computer base, I should be ready to start."

"Sounds like a mind-bender."

"It has its moments."

Ed plunked his cigar in the ashtray. "We'll have to get together sometime, the four of us. I'm sure we'd hit it off in no time." He cleared his throat. "I hate to cut this short, but my break is about over. I can let you see your friend for a few minutes, tops. The last thing I need is to get canned. Fran would have a fit."

"I understand. I won't be long."

"Oh, and not a word to the guards. They know what's up, but I need to keep everything simple and to the point."

Tim nodded as he hopped from the car. Ed tucked a few items under the front seat and locked up.

"Give me ten minutes, then be at the side entrance." Ed pointed, adjusted his belt, and headed in.

Tim glanced at Ed's outfit: navy-colored slacks, a sky-blue shirt, and black Rockport walkers—no hat, coat, or tie; those extras were for the guards at the main entrance. Ed vanished into the front of the Forensic Center, on his way to the third floor and dangerous criminals.

Built in the '40s, the Forensic Center reminded Tim of a small public grade school—rectangular, sandy-red brick, and awning windows. The faint odor of disinfectant lingers throughout the interior; the halls are echoey; the doors are sledgehammer heavy—and no elevators. Inmates wear street clothes and tennis shoes or cloth slippers. Watches, lightweight chains, and bracelets are permitted. Straitjackets are unnecessary. Hostile prisoners are met with force, a quick sedative, and isolation for however long it takes to tame the beast.

As the sun crept west Tim waited at the side entrance. Ed casually escorted him to the third floor. The echoes from their shoes clacking against the tile steps sounded like horses hooves. The first guard who spotted them winked, but wasn't the least bit interested in questioning them. Some inmates were napping, others were in the rec room down the hall. Doors to their cubicles were propped open. As Tim and Ed strolled through the central corridor, two guards nodded then ignored them. Ed had handled things smoothly.

The last thing Tim wanted was to blow what little time he had, but it couldn't be helped. He tapped Ed and asked to use the restroom. Ed thought for a second and nodded:

"Make it quick—there." He pointed to a battered door a few yards away. "I'll be down the hall. I'll signal to you when you come out. And hey, don't fall in." He chuckled.

Dim, fluorescent light gave the room a murky appearance. The squares of tile glistened like the underbelly of an alligator. Except for a leaky faucet, the only sound was faint echoes from down the hall. Feeling tense Tim quickly barged into a stall. As he sat there scanning the floor (his eyes tracing the shadows, subconsciously giving form to each one) something moved— the shadows grew. He cocked his head and flinched. A chilling image pierced the air, then vanished. Tim swore he heard someone running away. He was sure the restroom door opened and closed. "It couldn't be." He gasped. Had Robert been spying on him from the top of the stall? Tim shook himself and went to wash his hands. As he darted into the hall, Ed called to him. Ed's supervisor was due any minute.

"Come on," Ed grunted as they marched to the threshold of the cubical; then he whispered: "I don't think he knows we're here."

"Ya sure he hasn't been roaming the halls?" Tim couldn't help letting that out. The restroom vision lingered.

"I seriously doubt it; but why do you ask?" Ed snickered. "What'd he do, pay you a visit while you were squeezing a load?"

"Maybe." Tim waited for Ed to confirm his suspicion.

"Looks to me like he's been here all the time—see?" Ed's eyes shifted to the cubical.

Robert was alone, lying in bed, staring at the ceiling. Perhaps he was dazed; perhaps he was ill; but he was unquestionably in a world of his own. His lips were crinkled in a bizarre half-smile. He appeared to be dozing. Robert looked as Tim imagined: taller, though as slim for his size as when he was a child. His face was smooth, barely a wrinkle; his hair, the same mop-top bangs with a trace of gray. Other than an oversized nose, he looked strikingly similar to the Robert of Tim's childhood. His black corduroys and gray tennis shoes were eclipsed by a glossy T-shirt that screamed:

> SHOW ME YOUR VANILLA
> AND I'LL SHOW YOU MINE

Boy did that bring back memories.

Ed nudged Tim and winked. "Why don't you say 'hello'?"

"Wouldn't you be screwed if Robert told your boss I was here?"

"That's a hot one," Ed chortled softly. "His word against mine; but I can't let you talk to your wacko pal anyway. Though if circumstances were right I'd damn well let you BS with the creep all you wanted; and right now he's as alone as a flea on Uranus. His roommates are in the day room playing cards."

Tim gazed at Robert nestled in his dreary hollow. An uncanny longing propelled Tim to his childhood and the moment beneath the willows when his delirious playmate finished his nightmare. Robert had looked as drained as John, his prized shrunken head. Tim obsessed over the eerie faces Robert used to make. He and Sheri knew Robert was anything but normal. They often wondered whether he visited a shrink. Then there were the times Tim and Sheri asked if there was anything wrong, especially when Robert was in one of his trances. With a queer smile he'd gaze at the sky and chant: "Nothing, nothing's wrong, you see; and what could be wrong? Nothing, nothing with me." But the way he said it, in a sinister whisper, always gave them chills. Tim never asked Sheri how well she had slept the night Robert told his dream. Tim had slipped into the kitchen, grabbed a cleaver, and left it on his nightstand. He wasn't taking any chances.

"Ed, I heard that Robert murdered his parents—but how?"

He motioned Tim away. "All I know is that he butchered 'em fiendishly. I think he used an axe, or was it a hatchet? I can't remember for sure; but when the police found the bodies there was blood everywhere. I guess some freaks don't know when to clean house."

Following Ed back to the open door, Tim frowned at Robert, shook his head, and wondered: were Robert's parents demons? If Robert had only confided certain secrets . . . He lay smiling like a blood-bloated vampire.

You ever get the feeling when you're spying on someone that unexpectedly they'll twist their head until their eyes meet yours and smile ghoulishly? They know you're watching—like the ghastly brat from the *Exorcist* movie, leering at you with the scarred, swollen face, glassy eyes, and dog breath from hell.

Some people never change, Tim shivered. Robert in his own way had found freedom from all responsibility. As for Tim he had seen enough. He wasn't about to hang around until Robert's eyes locked with his, or Ed caught hell from his boss. Ed ushered him downstairs. "Take 'er easy—hope to get together soon." He pitched Tim a thumbs up.

Tim thanked him and exited into a picturesque afternoon. As he headed for his car, the steel-plated door to the Forensic Center creaked shut. Straining to erase Robert's visage from his thoughts, Tim considered how accommodating Ed had been and what future hijinks they might enjoy. He turned to view the sanitarium and surrounding grounds. His senses unfurled. The sun was perched on a grand horizon. Its harvest beams bestowed to the landscape a life of its own: surreal, beyond beauty, a vision so awe-inspiring Tim had to stop and drink from it. He imagined wading through a field of lush, earthy grass. Blackbirds whistled as he drifted to a golden sunset amidst radiant sapphire skies and marshmallow clouds. With each step into the shimmering vista he floated higher, as if he were entering a divine kingdom . . . Bewitched he faded departing to yesterday—his treasured memories and classic films: for a moment he yearned, as Ida Lupino had in Rod Serling's "Twilight Zone" episode "The 16 Millimeter Shrine," to eternally remain in the glorious past as a world famous celebrity hosting euphoric parties 'til doomsday . . .

Shaking his head Tim snapped to and wondered whether the place was a golf course for the angels; funny how a mental institution could afford the grounds such quality maintenance.

The next night Tim kept his promise and he and Cathy feasted while debating the news, their favorite movies, and their youth. The only topic they excluded was Robert.

Chapter 7

The Corvair sat vacant, anxious its passengers wouldn't return. From the royal-purple sky dark finger clouds slithered across the day-glow orange mid-summer moon. In the woods of Seminary Valley, east of Latham Street, near the hidden entrance, he gazed in awe. His face tingled to the night breeze. Once forgotten, so old its brand name had worn off, it had been discarded deep in a drawer bulging with junk—yet the second he held it and motioned, oh how it sang! Noise from the clearing ruffled his trance. Illuminated by flashlight they swayed to Grace Slick whose bewitching chant quivered from the cassette player. Sitting cross legged, toking and swigging and joking, rubbish spewed from their lips as he quietly made pentagrams in the earth. If only they'd leave.

"Naylor! You sure as hell fooled me." With a shit-happy grin Bish slapped the knees of his faded straight-leg Levis. "I thought you'd play 'White Rabbit' or 'Crown of Creation.' Azoo, give me the VG now!" He flexed his shoulders, grabbed the fifth of whiskey, swallowed, pitched it to Naylor, downed half a can of Schaefer and belched.

Even if "Lather" was an odd pick only Naylor would have added to the playlist, Bish appreciated it. As teens swiftly donning manhood, and their world not to be inhabited by those 30 and over, the song lulled and the lyrics felt right. Jefferson Airplane would be at Woodstock in a few weeks.

"What can I say, it beckoned." Naylor sipped and coughed. "Here, dude." He passed the bottle to Azoo.

"Bringing the tunes and player is cool." Bish sucked slowly, exhaled the Jamaican from his nose, and passed the joint to Naylor. "But if the bum-fuck neighbors didn't call the cops, I'd damn well park the Corvair in the woods and blast tunes from the 8-track—then we'd really rock!"

Glaring at them through elms from 20 feet away, he spotted the cassette player and nodded.

"Stuff's decent, but nothing like the Columbian we had a week ago." Naylor blinked at the tail end of a meteor and smiled at the moon. "Awesome—incredible! Apollo 11 only days ago, Armstrong & Aldrin kicking real moon dirt on TV—I was blown away. Captain Kirk here we come."

Azoo chuckled. "Star Trek may arrive sooner than we think."

"I can only wonder what the '70s will be like, not to mention 2000 and beyond." Bish sighed. "Hey, 'Lather' was good, but brighten it up. Great! This one works." He nudged Naylor as "The Ballad Of John And Yoko" blared from his best friend's portable.

Banging acoustic guitar with a rocked down "Don't Be Cruel" bass line, closet-echo vocals, punchy drums, and clipped spasms of lead guitar: some radio stations refused to air the notorious ode because of its cheeky reference to Christ.

Naylor jerked out a Winston: "Wonder when pot'll be legal?"

"Not in our lifetimes."

"Come on, Bish; what about in 10 or 20 years?"

"Too many old farts screwing with the US; though eventually the tide may turn. If we could ship The Establishment to Vietnam before our numbers hit, and then can the draft—"

They hung their heads wishing war never existed.

"Now that Nixon's finally pulling out troops, we may luck out of being forced into that cesspool." Naylor passed the joint to Azoo. "Then we wouldn't be zombie soldier fuckups digging our tombs."

"Speaking of old farts screwing with things," Bish tightened the knot of his jean jacket sleeves around his waist. "How 'bout Dennis Hopper getting blown off his Harley by shotgun rednecks? What a movie! I wouldn't mind us touring the US or Canada in choppers."

"Easy Rider was a trip." Naylor finished his beer and popped open another. "Which reminds me: one of these days you've got to get experienced—have you ever been? as Hendrix put it."

"Maybe I'll fly when I'm in college. I've got enough buzzing in my brain to start tripping now."

"It's weird and warped and sometimes wild, but what a rush."

"Ya ought to try it once, Bish?" Azoo rubbed his palms. "Naylor and I did it twice—an awesome psychedelic ride!"

Bish shook his fist at Azoo. "Shut up or you'll get a ride. I'll pulverize your ass."

Naylor parted his hands. "I hear you, Bish. Do it when you're ready and not a second sooner. Acid is a grave adventure. One never knows who will flip out and go suicidal. Although I wouldn't mind suicide. Give me the right drugs, a touch of booze, and sweet car exhaust in a closed garage. It'd be a breeze. I often dream of ways I'll die and how great the aftermath: no more idiots to deal with, no more school rules and jackass teachers, no more violence and Vietnam and having to fight for a phony cause—how 'bout that? No harassment and no pain . . . a new beginning."

"You are bizarre." Bish shook his head. "Unbelievable you're wired the way you are."

Naylor pointed at Azoo. "Ya should have gone with us."

"What?" Azoo was spacing out.

"To Easy Rider."

"Shit!" Azoo blinked. "That was the night my old man forced me to hang and BS with his and mom's dear friends— what a drag. I was spazzing to join you!" Azoo dropped the end of the joint into an empty beer can, which he tossed into the trees. "Got three fingers of Virginia Gentleman left; any takers?"

Bish shook his head. "I'm fucked up just right—don't want to blow the perfect high."

"Finish it, Azoo." Naylor solemnly clicked off his player. "The next one is for Brian, released just weeks ago, the day after he . . . one hellacious music guru now in rock heaven; to us he'll never fade away."

Bish was dying to shout how Jagger and Richards were the true geniuses—they were the Stones! But when he realized Naylor's sorrow, he kicked back and smiled riding the ripples of his buzz.

Ticks from a cowbell—the bap, bam, boom of Charlie's drums—and Keith's raucous open-G-tuned Les Paul fuel injected Mick's sleazy vocal.

Scowling in the dark he donned rubber gloves, flexed his fingers, and cringed when they sang to the chorus of "Honkey Tonk Women"—raunch to his ears.

"I heard 'PGC first play it a week ago—great tune!" Azoo sipped his bourbon.

"Yep, it's slowly catching." Naylor leaned back against a tree trunk. "WEAM and WEEL are also airing it."

"What the hell." Bish glared at Azoo. "One more swig— give it." He took half a chug, nodded at Naylor who shook his head, then capped it and tossed it back to Azoo. "We appreciate the booze, Azoo, which reminds me: you know at first I couldn't put my finger on it." Bish clapped. "But now I know what's different about tonight."

"Yeah?" Azoo and Naylor replied in stereo.

"You guys decided to act civil. Perhaps Azoo's brother letting you record his albums and 45s onto cassette didn't hurt."

Naylor nodded. "It's also phenomenal that Azoo's brother is allowing us passage to Woodstock via his Dodge wagon." He stared at Bish. "Seriously, are you joining us?"

"Yeah, Bish." Azoo lit another joint, puffed and passed it to Naylor. "All for none or none at all?" He raised his beer to silence.

Bish gazed through the treetops at a distant star before replying. "I'm not stoked about cruising in the rear of a packed Polara, much less listening to Azoo's brother's friends' dumbass remarks all the way to New York and back, which is at least a five to six hour trek each way."

"Excuses." Naylor growled then dragged deeply on his Winston.

"Alright, I wanna go, and the cramped car isn't an issue; but you know the deal with my dad."

"What does his chipping in half on a new GTO if you keep your grades up have to do with going to Woodstock?" Naylor snorted.

"You were always book smart; grades are no sweat—hell, you must get off on reading." Bish squinted. "I struggle with every subject except no-nonsense math. Homework sucks—it takes me hours to finish. But here's the real deal: with his negative attitude about the concert, I figure if I go there's a chance he'll bail out of the deal."

"You'd trade freedom to rock for a materialistic teenage status symbol? Fuck that shit!"

Bish tore off a clump of grass, pumped it with his fist, closed his eyes for a brief moment, and nodded. "Naylor, you're absolutely right. I won't say a word, just go to Woodstock—then, if he cops out, screw him and my grades."

"Don't sweat the marks, I'll help you; if anyone can, I can—that's a promise." Naylor smiled, especially because he knew how much Bish loved what had just pounced from his player. Pete Townshend's chucky guitar intro to "Go to the Mirror!"

As the song unfurled, Bish nodded. "Shit, watching footage from Monterey, they blew me away! Pete annihilated his guitar and Moon kicked the shit out of his drums—what a finale!"

"Woodstock, yeah!" Azoo shook his fists and shouted. "Hendrix, Joplin, Airplane, Creedence, Canned Heat, the Who—Bish, you love the Who! You gotta go, man."

"Hell, I'm in!" Bish laughed.

They all popped open beers and toasted. Azoo tossed the last of the whiskey to Bish who downed it and chucked the bottle into the pines.

Azoo stared suspiciously at the surrounding woods.

"What's up?" Naylor tapped him. "Something wrong?"

"Tonight something's off, out of whack. I didn't mention it at first because we were having a great time, but—"

"Don't start that shit again!" Bish kicked dirt at Azoo.

Naylor glared. "The same vibes you dished out the time we found the head in the woods. Whatever or whoever you think is watching, we can whip ass, so stop being a pussy, chill and enjoy!"

Bish shook his head. "For the first time in months you and Naylor were riding a friend groove. But with you, Azoo, it never lasts: you always weird out or fuck up—what the hell's your problem?"

"You always give me shit. What about Naylor? He's weird."

"Asshole!" Naylor smacked Azoo's shoulder. "Don't start—"

"Naylor may be weird, but he's entertaining and likeable. You, Azoo, are annoying and unintelligent, plus you always screw up things—like busting the stem off of Naylor's new bong and shattering his black light."

"You had to remind me." Naylor rolled his eyes.

"Not to mention the hole you burned in the Corvair seat."

"They're accidents anyone could have done." Azoo spat to the side. "I did pay for the seat."

Bish tipsily leapt to his feet. "I'm takin' a leak and when I return you better have made up or someone's ass is getting kicked; and I can tell you without a doubt it won't be Naylor's."

Azoo apologized to Naylor.

"Don't sweat it, everything's cool." Naylor nodded.

Azoo guzzled his beer and started to relax as Bish parted the pines, stepped ten paces into the woods, turned and began to piss.

"Hey Bish?" Naylor started the next song. "I hear they'll also be at Woodstock."

The ghostly electric 12-string to "Guinevere" seeped dreamily from the player. Mystic Crosby, Stills, and Nash harmonies enchanted the woods.

"Crank it!" Bish shouted . . . The booze, the pot, the surreal moon; visions of The Who at Woodstock; Bish singing to his girlfriend, Jan, whom he imagined as the radiant maiden, Guinevere—he was beyond heaven! Oblivious he zipped up his fly and was stunned.

"One," rip, "two," rip, "three," rip—fiendishly he slashed to Bish's screams. "Scum, bastard!" He whispered and quickly departed.

Bish fell to his knees, slapped the earth face first, turned and buckled into a fetal position. His body surged, his eyes expanded, pain soared, shock struck. He cocked his head to the swirl and glow of the woods and sky and moon. From his daze, as he retched for his life, his friends rushed to him. His eyes closed. He faded . . .

Sitting in a lotus position, underwater, at the bottom of the deep end of his swimming pool, dressed in Their Satanic Majesties Request regalia, Brian cradled his sitar. Pale eyes and skin and purple lips pulsated to his wavering mop top. Bubbles burst from his mouth, but Bish couldn't make out the words, just gargling, until Brian plugged a set of headphones into the body of the sitar and handed them to Bish.

"Come to where the flavor is, man; join in. The real Stones died with me. What's left is an illusion. This is reality. Ah ha ha ha!"

Brian's face morphed into Naylor's as Bish briefly regained consciousness. The voice next to Naylor sounded like Azoo's.

"Shit look, we gotta do something!"

"Careful, Azoo." Naylor shuddered as he aimed the flashlight at Bish's back.

"I'll get it—damn!" Azoo grunted as he fell on his ass.

"Don't kill him!" Naylor clasped the handle and pulled, but his fingers were slick and the knife remained.

"Fu-fuck!" Bish groaned.

Azoo gently tugged. "Finally!" He sighed and pitched the weapon high into the trees.

They failed to notice the click from the cassette player and the music stopping.

Bish heaved as he hallucinated to warped visions of the famous: some living, some recently deceased . . .

Tricky Dick sported a gaudy Hawaiian shirt and white swimming trunks. With a Luger to his head, he flashed the peace sign and smirked. "Riddle me this, son: how many dead presidents does it take to run the country or end the war? Sock it to me!" . . .

From the stark rural roadside, shotgun bloodied Easy Rider Billy's eyes flickered as he gasped. "I'm bleedin', Bish. Help me, man!" . . .

Sitting side by side, dressed in white, serenely holding hands, John and Yoko smiled. Lennon bobbed his head. "Bish, ya know it ain't easy. But do you really know how hard life can be?"

For a moment he surfaced to his friends. Azoo yanked a Winston from Naylor's shirt pocket, lit, and puffed.

"Fuck, run to a phone and call emergency!" Tears trickled down Naylor's cheeks.

"Right." Azoo snapped out of his trance and stomped the cigarette. "Try to hold it together, please." He dashed out of sight as Naylor started to unravel.

Twice Azoo fell tearing his jeans and scraping both knees. As he scrambled around the east end of Shirley Duke Shopping Center, he spotted the dimly lit phone booth and burst inside. Panting he pawed into his pockets, but no coins. "Hell!" He kicked the glass enclosure, which jarred the receiver, and to his ears droned the dial tone. He sighed remembering the recent change: callers could now reach an operator without inserting a dime. He pounded 0 and yelled for help. Azoo settled down after the operator explained that she couldn't understand what he was saying. As best he could Azoo communicated the specifics. Shell shocked he exited the booth, staggered to the front of Drug Fair and leaned back against the white brick. He blinked at the Grand Union where his mother bought the family groceries—a favorite haunt when he had the munchies— and where hours ago with a fake ID he purchased beer; then he gazed at Waxie Maxie's contemplating the hours he combed the record bins for great deals and weird releases. Azoo felt decent about the call and hopeful Bish would pull through; and then he remembered. "Shit!" He paced quickly and then ran—imagining what the police would find and what conclusions they'd reach after they arrived: the booze, beer, pot, and weapon with his and Naylor's fingerprints. What if Bish died?"

Naylor sobbed as he tried to comfort Bish who wheezed, his body heaving like an epileptic, sinking deeper and deeper to . . .

Ike was on his deathbed at Walter Reed Army Medical Center pleading for morphine. And from the dim doorway, in a nurse's uniform, peered the frail, barbiturate laden Judy Garland. Nervously she entered the room and with a raspy whisper replied.

"Mr. President, Sir? All I seem to have are these." She shook the bottle of sedatives and blinked. "But I was able to get you your gin and tonic, here." She handed Dwight his libation."

"My angel of mercy." He grinned. "Thank you, my dear."

Judy turned to Bish and popped a few before giving the bottle to Ike. And from her morose face flitted a plea for freedom from her neuroses.

"Care to join us, Son?" The decrepit commander and chief smiled.

Judy's lips twitched. "Yes, we'd love to take you with us. We're finally going o— . . . beyond the rainbow." With a weary smile she began to sing, then paused. "They say it's heavenly. Oh won't you join us?"

Total darkness and then it ended. Naylor shivered uncontrollably over his best friend's corpse.

Chapter 8

Six months after his visit to Pittsburgh, Tim received an unexpected call. It seemed as if a century had passed since he had spoken to any of the Riddicks.

"How'd you find me?" He pounded the kitchen table, ecstatic. "My number's been unpublished for years."

"Yesterday I was at Southcenter Mall with a close friend who mentioned you in connection with an appraisal her company was updating and—"

"Sheri!" Tim bolted from his chair. "What are you doing in Seattle?"

"I live in North Hills."

South of Sea-Tac Airport, the North Hills section of Des Moines, Washington, is a reputable middle-class suburb of split-level homes with a decent view of Puget Sound.

"When did you arrive?"

"About 20 years ago, with Mom and Dad. My brothers left Northern Virginia years before we moved."

"You remember in junior high school we used to write to each other?"

"That plus numerous long-distance calls."

"It's been ages since I've seen the old neighborhood. I miss you, Sheri."

"Me too. I was crushed when you moved."

"Really?" Revved by the possibility of renewing their relationship, Tim glowed. "I knew you liked me, but I thought I was the one with the crush."

"I used to dream that someday we'd start our life, but we stopped writing and calling a few years after you left. High school must have consumed us—all our new friends and responsibilities. Time rearranges things. I tried calling you when I first arrived, but information had no listing. Then I tried your parents, and some idiot answered who said that the phone number had been his for years. I figured you moved out of state."

Tim buckled with regret. "I was in San Diego for six months visiting Mom and checking the job scene—never did stay."

"How is your mom? I remember how nicely she treated me. I hope she's okay. I also remember you telling me that your father passed away. He was a decent man. He reminded me of Robert Young from *Father Knows Best*."

"Mom's fine; she remarried, to a classmate of Dad's; and Dad . . . I was fourteen when he died. I've had plenty of time to accept it. I really miss him, though. We never talked man-to-man. He used to shake his head, puzzled over how I could watch the same movie again and again. If he were here today I'd tell him that if a picture or painting is worth a thousand words, then to me a great film, which is a vast collage of images, is worth infinitely more; and until a time machine is invented, watching quality films that meticulously recreate the past, or films created years ago (contemporary when released) utterly fascinates me: I feel I'm in the past as a ghost able to observe how life used to be. I'd like to sit with Dad over a few beers—he liked Falstaff—and update him on my life. I guess he knows I made it, everything worked out, and eventually I grew up . . . as much as can be expected. I couldn't have asked for a better father. Dad, wherever you are, I'll see you soon enough. Save us a corner booth and a pitcher of draft. I'm sorry," Tim felt awkward over his impromptu burst of sentimentality. "I didn't mean to bring you down. You were telling me about when you first hit town."

"That's okay," she cooed. "I know you loved your father. I love mine—don't know what I'll do when he and Mom pass away. As I was saying, after I arrived I tried to contact you, but you were in San Diego. Time passed and I met Dan."

"Who?" A jolt of angst forced Tim to brace himself.

"My husband, Dan Davis." She said it so blissfully. "We were married in June of '85. It was a small wedding, just immediate family." Her voice echoed.

Tim had always believed sooner or later they'd be together, but life manipulates: things get screwed up, you mature, you forge your career, and before you know it, wham—middle-age.

"I'm happy for you." Bullshit, Tim was disappointed and pissed. He could have kicked himself for not keeping in touch, especially after hearing she'd moved—man, was he an idiot. This would've been the perfect time for a permanent relationship with a woman he truly cared about. From the recesses of his trampled heart, Tim felt he had lost his soulmate. Her voice intruded:

"No kids. Dan and I—you'd really like him; we decided that not having children is the best way to survive—besides we have a boatload of nieces and nephews. What about you?"

Tim's head exploded: Like Dan, my ass! I'd like him all right—enough to kick the living shit out of him and steal Sheri away. Tim tried to ignore the bomb she had detonated. He perked up. What a phony act that was.

"There were plenty of opportunities for marriage, but I never found the right mate; you know how it goes."

"I suppose, though I thought for sure you'd be married and have a few kids."

"Things don't always go as planned." He reached into the refrigerator and grabbed a cold Amstel.

"Guess I got lucky." She quickly changed the subject. "Are you still into classic movies? Nice to have TCM. There's nothing better than chilling to Joan Crawford or Bette Davis, you know, like *Mildred Pierce* or *All About Eve*."

"How 'bout *What Ever Happened to Baby Jane?*"

"Yeah!" Sheri cleared her throat. "Bette literally kicks the crap out of Joan—I believe she purposely called for a few retakes of the scene just for spite, who knows?"

"And Bette serving Joan baked parakeet and then rat."

"Disgusting—and how Bette cackled when Joan groaned."

"So many phenomenal films," Tim chugged a third of his beer and suppressed a belch. "Like *Key Largo* and *Treasure of Sierra Madre*: great characters and stories—Robinson, Bogart, Bacall, Lionel Barrymore, Claire Trevor, Walter Huston; hell, Tim Holt's character reminds me of some of my college buddies."

"Speaking of John Huston movies, I recently saw a 1960s flick starring Richard Burton—I was howling; Burton was a scream and Ava Gardner wonderful in *Night of the Iguana*."

"Burton's portrayal of the henpecked priest is hilarious. He and Liz—they could have made some blockbuster comedies."

"What about work?"

Tim finished his beer and set the empty on the counter. "As you know, I'm a commercial real estate appraiser. I have an office downtown and an efficient crew. I also teach the subject."

"That's a far cry from what you wanted when we were kids. Remember at the pool, your dreams of being a scientist or an archaeologist? What happened?"

"Changes and reality." Eager to slam his fist through the wall, he popped open another brew. "What about you? I remember you were going to be a pilot or doctor . . . well?"

Her disillusionment seeped through the receiver. "I passed on those, though I do aid people. I'm a career counselor for those who are unsure of their talents and can't figure what best suits them."

"I could have used you when I was in my twenties. Man was I a mess—didn't have a clue what to do. What about Mike and Dave?"

Sheri's brother, Mike, who Tim knew casually, had toiled for years as a patent attorney; he now owns a Harley Davidson store—all the years of straight work had sparked the rebel in him. Dave, one of Tim's childhood heroes, operates "Nostalgia Sync!" a company that specializes in picture-perfect reunions providing fabulous environments faithfully reminiscent of the time and place where each group used to socialize. As she finished updating Tim he realized, regardless of his reluctance to forgive her for marrying, how much he missed Sheri and her family. Tim mentioned his trip to Pittsburgh and the shocking news. He was curious whether she had heard about it.

"You mean the blood bath!" She bellowed. "One of Robert's cronies informed my best friend months after it happened."

Tim was all ears as she disclosed the gory details. It was like a repeat of Robert's nightmare. Apparently without warning he went berserk. In an act of demented rage, Robert hacked his parents to pieces. And where did the police find the remains? In the freezer, of course. But that wasn't the worst of it.

"Well," Sheri hesitated. "When they opened the freezer there was more than your typical bloody remnants. The officers' stomachs must have flipped in disgust. Bulging from the mouths of Robert's mother and father were their genitals. Robert had severed his father's penis and scrotum, with testicles intact, and sewed them to his lips. He did the same with his mother's vagina."

Tim dropped the receiver and retched. Dumbfounded by Robert's depravity Tim wondered what a top-notch psychiatrist would conclude. As he snatched the receiver Sheri asked if he was okay.

"Barely," he strained.

The motive for Robert's repulsive deed would likely remain a mystery. Tim and Sheri knew he was a screwball, but they never imagined his life would detour so hideously. If they'd known him better (gotten closer, kept the lines of communication open) they might've saved him from the talons of ruin. Sheri continued:

"You know, Robert's behavior didn't surprise me. After you left, before he and his parents moved to Pittsburgh, I started to worry."

"Go on." Tim quivered.

"The few times I saw him, I noticed a change. I know you liked him, though not on the level he liked you. I could tell, the times the three of us were together, by the way he acted and by his body language, that he thought the world of you; yet he was sure you deliberately deserted him when you left for Seattle."

"I was twelve. I had to move. What did Robert expect me to do, tell my folks to fuck off, then stay here and sleep wherever until I found a job? Sorry to be crude, but it often frustrates me the way people act."

"I know exactly how you feel; but you know how screwed up and insecure he was. You and I were his only friends, especially you; so when you left I guess he was traumatized."

"That's not my fault. I'm not his father. When I tried calling him long-distance, he'd either hang up, or his parents would say he was too busy to come to the phone. But wait, you started to worry—about?"

"He always insisted I go out with him. He needed love and friendship. As reluctant as I was to see him, I tried to be nice. Occasionally, on a weekend, we'd spend an hour, but only during the day. I didn't feel safe with him at night. We'd talk about old times and he'd try to get romantic, holding my hand and telling me how nice I was and how happy he was to see me. I tried to keep a straight face. I felt sorry for him; but I wasn't about to lead him on, so I'd firmly tell him to stop fooling around. He'd let go of my hand, and then from the clear blue break into his weird routine: you know, he'd start quoting from an old horror movie, and when I nudged him he'd stare at the sky and chant, 'Nothing, nothing's wrong you see; and what could be wrong? Nothing, nothing with me.' It was just too much. After a few afternoons I stopped seeing him."

"Then what?"

"Strange things . . . like when I'd pass him on the street. He'd gaze at me with a perverted smile. When I ignored him he'd act like he was going to kill me. One time he yanked out a switchblade and made slashing gestures."

"Did you tell your parents or brothers?"

"I thought it best to handle things myself. Besides, I felt sorry for him. If he had gone haywire I would've told someone. No use upsetting my family unless it was absolutely necessary."

"But Sheri, you have to nip those things in the bud."

"Anyway, two months before he moved to Pittsburgh, I started getting obscene phone calls."

"Oh boy; how'd you know it was him?"

"Come on, he wasn't trying hard to fake his voice. You remember how he sounded, always in that low, whispery tone."

"How could I forget; I can hear him now, like on the night he told us his crazy dream. But you were saying—what obscenities?"

"Things I'd rather not repeat; they were gross, sexual, and cruel. I tried to reason with him saying, 'Robert, I know it's you. Please don't call anymore.' But he continued his vulgar ranting: always telling me how much he wanted me and how sooner or later he would have his way."

"It's hard to imagine Robert behaving so maliciously towards you."

"There's more."

"Huh?" Tim massaged the goose bumps on his neck.

"Oh yes. Every so often when I was combing my hair, getting ready for bed, I'd get the feeling someone was spying on me from the backyard. I'd rush to the window and peek out . . . nothing. Then I'd listen carefully. I swear I heard the faint footsteps of someone running away.

"One summer night I spotted him. As I was getting undressed I moved quietly to the window and peered out. He was in the middle of the yard, like Count Dracula; something gleamed in his hands. I'm sure it was a knife. He saw me, but didn't run, just uttered his desire: 'Sheri—Sheri! I need you. You will be mine. Never forget, Sheeerrrriiii!' Trembling, I slammed the window shut. He scurried across the backyard and hopped the chain-link fence. 'That's it!' I raised a fist. 'If he does it again I'll tell Mike and Dave, and they'll annihilate him.' But that never happened. Robert moved and everything settled down. Once or twice a year I'd get one of his sick phone calls; but with time that ended. I guess the long-distance expense was too much; either that or he found a new hobby."

"Yep, disposing of his parents. But why, when we were writing each other, didn't you tell me those things?" Tim felt a mule kick to his ego. "All you said was that Robert was being a pain and you were trying your best to ignore him."

"I didn't want you to worry. Even though the thought of you returning was incredible, it would have been ruined if you were coming just to punish Robert, so I barely mentioned it in my letters. I figured if he laid a hand on me I'd let everyone know."

"But that's waiting too long. God, I'm relieved he never hurt you. After what he did to his parents, consider yourself damn lucky."

"I do, believe me."

"Speaking of his parents—" Tim paused to polish off his beer. "Did Robert ever tell you what they were really like?"

"You remember how he was. Details regarding his parents were definitely taboo. I think he relished keeping his vile secrets to himself. Though I wonder about his mother and father. Maybe they beat and tortured him, who knows. All I remember Robert saying—and you were there to hear it—was that his dad owned a carpet business and his mom was an ordinary housemom. He always said that with stoic pride."

"I doubt they were the torturing type. They barely paid attention to us, the time or two we saw them. I can't believe they'd intentionally abuse their son."

"Worse things have happened."

"Maybe so. Hey, you remember Robert mentioning his hideout, where he wandered to when he was depressed? He fixed it up like a tree fort and treated it like a second home."

"Yeah and I remember how you and I searched for it all those weekends. It was fun at first, but then it became a pain."

"Did he ever tell you where it was?"

"Now that you mention it . . . though it wasn't a tree fort. It was sort of underground. I think he said that it was inside a small hill. After you moved he asked me a million times if I would go there, and I always turned him down. I wasn't about to be cooped up with him in his hideout, much less fight him off when he got nasty notions."

"You were damn smart not to."

"Let me see, if I remember correctly, Robert told me it was off of Latham Street—now it's coming to me—near the bottom of Latham, on the left where the woods are, at the edge of a clearing, I think."

"Between our neighborhood and Shirley Duke Shopping Center?"

"Right, only now it's called Foxchase."

"Where? What clearing?"

"I'm trying to remember. It's on the tip of my tongue."

"Relax. Try to picture it."

"It's no good. It'll come to me, though, and when it does I'll let you know, I promise. But why after all these years are you interested? I'm sure there's nothing there; but if there is it's bound to be rotted or withered to dust."

"Probably, but aren't you curious what you might find?"

"No. My life's fine, thank you. I've paid my dues trying to rehabilitate Robert after you left. I tried to reason with him, and what good did it do? I don't need any grim reminders to depress me. But go ahead if you like. You were closer to him than I ever was. Try to find the place if it makes you happy . . . I almost forgot about the incident that happened in the woods near Robert's hideout: very sinister how one of the teenagers died. His buddies were convicted and served time."

"What?" Tim scratched his head. "Wait, I remember shortly after I moved, you mentioned it in one of your letters. They were the high school kids I saw at Hammond cafeteria the day I delivered your brother's homework assignment."

"The leader, I believe his name was Bish, was stabbed to death in late July of '69."

"Right! And based on weapon fingerprints, they convicted the other two, Naylor and Azoo."

"Addison Zooder was his full name; but I can't help wondering if Robert was involved."

"Robert might have murdered Bish if Bish and his friends discovered the hideout."

"Weird, because when I mentioned the incident to my girlfriend, she stated that when she asked one of Robert's cronies (whom she was dating) whether Robert had murdered Bish, he replied, 'No way.' But the nervousness in his voice suggested he may have been lying; though I'm sure for good reason—Robert was a master at revenge."

"What about Naylor and Azoo?" Tim pulled another Amstel from the fridge.

"Depressing. Robert never got to either of them, though his vengeance was fulfilled. It was a shame Naylor went to prison. I heard he was highly intelligent; though once behind bars he figured it best when released to continue with crime. There was a robbery shoot out—he never left the bank alive."

"Wow! And Azoo?"

"Believe it or not he was helping his girlfriend kick heroin when he was clubbed to death by an angry dealer who had been shorted money. Azoo attempted in vain to pay the dealer whose rule was to kill first and ask questions later."

"That's dismal."

"I will call you if I remember more details about his hideout."

"Sheri, you know the wild dream he told us under the willows?"

"Where he found my family murdered? How could I forget? Sometimes I wonder whether he purposely concocted it to belittle and annoy me. I could have slugged him when he mentioned Honey in the bread box. What about the dream?"

"Things he described in your parent's house: I don't remember——"

"I thought I told you, but apparently not. *You* know my father, and *you* visited our home countless times when we were kids. In Robert's dream he mentioned Dad's workshop and the ice chest downstairs. My father never had a workshop, and our only refrigerator/freezer was in the kitchen. Robert was never inside my parent's house."

"Really?" Tim's lips twitched.

"Every time the three of us played, we were at your house or outside."

"Then I guess the interior décor in his dream was, as we used to say when we were kids, 'a Fig Newton of his imagination.'"

"You remember how he loved horror books and movies. I'm sure it was easy for him to make believe anything. Besides, it was a dream, which reminds me: remember the night—about a week before Robert told us his dream—you and I were sitting on your parents' front stoop, just about twilight, and that black car went by?"

"Vaguely." Tim scratched his cheek.

"You remember the car Robert's strange acquaintance used to drive."

"That's right, screwy looking. I think it was a Plymouth Valiant. When I asked Robert about the guy, he denied everything as though his friend, or whoever it was, never existed."

"It had to be his psychiatrist."

"Makes sense to me." Tim shrugged. "Why else would Robert's parents let a stranger chauffeur their son."

"But that night—don't you remember the driver?"

"I wasn't paying attention."

"Someone else was at the wheel, some other man. I think it was Robert's father. All I know is that it wasn't the owner of the car. And there's another thing: on the rear of the vehicle someone had painted an inscription. I'm not sure what it said. Guess I was more interested in who was driving."

"I don't remember an inscription. Maybe it had always been there, and we just didn't notice it until you saw it."

"Maybe." Sheri's voice softened. "Tim, if you do search for his fort, please be careful. We had an incredible childhood; and now that we've reconnected, I'd hate to lose you."

There was a glow of sympathy in her voice: a feeling that though they disagreed about certain issues, with sisterly kindness she understood and supported Tim. He wanted her beside him. He wanted to stroke her curls and tell her how much he missed and loved her. It's a damn shame she's married, he winced.

Sheri rattled off her family's addresses and phone numbers. Tim assured her he'd stop by; though he wondered because of his slight jealousy toward Dan if he'd keep his promise.

Tim was truly amazed by Sheri's revelations. That bewitching night decades ago under the willow would forever define him. But wait—something clicked in his head: Sheri's description of Robert's parents' genitals sewn to their mouths. That's right! The day Tim skipped 6th grade recess to drop off Dave Riddick's assignment, Naylor had mentioned stitches around the mouth of the head he and his friends found. That sounded like Robert's handiwork; but he was too young to . . . or was he? Tim pictured Bish, Azoo, and Naylor debating what the initials on the bag, R & J, stood for. The R could easily have been Robert, but what did the J stand for?

Tim's gaze shifted from the oak grain of the kitchen table to the wavering shadows beyond the bay window. A bittersweet femme fatale from his college days twinkled in the recesses of his heart. Like Sheri, Maureen Rhodes was radiantly beautiful, yet she possessed a completely different personality. From the twilight her spirit beckoned.

Chapter 9

S he was casually sprawled on her brother's bed when Tim paid the dorm a routine visit. The instant he glimpsed her enchanting eyes, sleepy smile, ivory cheeks, silky locks, and a body that forced him to bite his knuckles, he was hooked—like a kid on candy he'd have to have a taste every chance he got. And so it was fortunate that her parents' house, where she spent much time, was a 15-minute drive from campus.

In September of '75 Tim and Maureen indulged in an incredible rendezvous that every so often his mind would replay like the bittersweet climax of a favorite movie . . .

The moon above her parents' home dazzled his senses. He leaped from the bucket seat of the Datsun 240Z and kicked the door shut. The coupe's silver sheen rippled to the moonlight. For a moment he ogled the front lawn, savoring the moist air, until the urge spurred him to pop a Salem to his pucker. Unfurling from his first drag his eyes glistened . . . mmm, nothing like being 19. He leaned against the 'Z and reminisced about high school. Crunching his smoke into the damp earth, he looked up and there she was with a dizzy smile, the kind you get as they put you under at the dentist's office.

"Hey," she looped her slender arms around his waist and zapped him with a zesty kiss that made him smile like he was in the dentist's chair.

"What are you doin' tonight, Big Boy?" She hailed in her best Mae West impression. "Got any plans?"

"You bet." Tim chuckled. "And tonight I'm surprising you with something capital."

"Ya gonna tell me?" Maureen sighed as she gently massaged his neck.

Before he could reply she spotted the car: undeniably sleek and sporty.

"This can't be yours unless you were gambling and hit the jackpot. If this is our 'wheels' tonight, well all right!" She shook her hips and pitched Tim a thumbs up.

"Yeah, though it belongs to a college buddy. I have it out on loan. Hop in." Tim fired open the passenger's door and glimpsed her sultry shape sink into the supple upholstery. He darted around and jumped in.

"Look at that dashboard," she whistled, "lights up like a Christmas tree; and the 8-track—cool. How fast will she go?"

"The owner told me, when he was on the interstate it did 120 easily." Tim revved the feisty 5-speed and squealed out.

"Better not let me behind the wheel. I might wreck it."

"I don't know. Driving a stick shift is like anything else. It takes practice. Bet I could teach you." Tim popped the clutch into third gear.

"Maybe," she nibbled his ear.

Maureen, an artist who painted avant-garde scenes in unusual watercolors, was a product of the late-sixties psychedelic scene: too many LSD trips, too many Grateful Dead concerts, and a visit to Haight-Ashbury in its heyday when she was a teenage runaway. Tim was amazed that the drugs and roller-coaster lifestyle hadn't defiled her looks. She was radiant with a childlike voice that belied her experiences. Besides, Tim peered beyond the drugs and hippie high ideals and perceived a sensitive, creative, and loving mate whom he sincerely cherished. She realized his infatuation and tried not to take advantage. She seemed to relish having a romantic, sexual relationship, though she wasn't in love. He felt she needed him to balance her life.

Maureen popped loose a button on Tim's shirt and fondled his chest. She knew that would get him going.

"What did ya bring tonight?" She purred deliciously against his cheek.

"Want some candy little girl?" He laughed as they screeched to a stop sign.

"Any you can dish out." She cocked her head and boldly licked her lips.

"I have two types. The one down here I'm saving for later." He pointed to his crotch as he tugged a pint of cognac from his jacket. "Here's to dreams." He passed the liquor.

With delicate, ivory-colored hands she raised the bottle and sipped. "Mmm, thanks."

Tim whisked the 'Z to downtown Boston and suitable parking. He cut the engine and they sat quietly.

"So where are we headed?" Her eyelashes flickered.

"On a tour of the city in a horse-drawn coach." He waited for his reply to register.

"You *do* make me smile . . . first cognac, and now this. I don't know what to say, but—" she winked mischievously and showered him with moist kisses.

They nuzzled and hugged and caught their breaths.

"I'm crazy for you." Tim caressed her forehead.

"Um hmm," she sighed.

Settling back they gazed at the stars. Maureen nodded. Her eyes turned glassy. He waited before rousing her.

"You okay?" He squeezed her shoulders. "Do you hear me?"

She smiled serenely as if she were meditating. Tim snapped his fingers and an inner force jolted her. Her eyes glittered like before. She pecked Tim's cheek and whispered, "I'm ready."

He escorted Maureen to their harbinger, a stately black coach with gold trim and vintage lanterns. Tim was delighted that it was enclosed. This would ensure an intimate ride. As they skipped across the last stretch of pavement—carefree, champing at passion's gates—their laughter echoed against the aging skyscrapers.

"Hullo," bid the lanky cabby with muttonchops, a top hat, and a suit that matched his coach. "John Tolbert at your service." He bowed graciously and opened the door. "You're my last ride for the evening." He assured them they'd be comfortable, have the utmost privacy, and he'd take an extra turn around town to make their trip truly rewarding. As Tim ushered Maureen inside, he slipped John a tip.

The seats were royal-blue velvet, the curtains, snow-white lace. John asked if they were secure before promising those would be his last words.

"Onward!" Tim chimed with a Cheshire cat grin.

They sailed through Boston, the urban din playing second fiddle to the clippity-clop of lively hooves. Tim and Maureen savored a toast of cognac before letting go. Oohing lustfully she pressed him to the corner, parted his shirt, and buried her face in his chest, nuzzling and licking it. He moaned as his fingers sailed across her shoulders to undo her dress. The motion of her body was so smooth he nearly burst. From his gentle tugging at the rear of her bra, it popped to the sides rendering her supple back. Tim delicately massaged Maureen's shoulders before straying below, his longing primed. He whispered how beautiful she was and how he adored her as she sucked on his chest and kneaded his neck: misty glow from a radiant siren savoring his flesh. Raising her lips to his, their tongues frolicked in a fiery kiss. Peeling his shirt away she shimmied from her dress and they flared to a primal blaze: moist lips smearing smooth skin. Beneath Tim's briefs her velvety fingers sailed, gently fondling the jewels of his groin; and with the finesse of a matador she whisked away his slacks and briefs. He stroked her gleaming locks as she bobbed hungrily, her supple lips churning 'round the throbbing core of his drive. Seconds before releasing he whispered for her to stop, then held her in his arms.

As the autumn moonlight flooded their sanctum, Maureen lay on lush velvet; her ebony eyes shimmered; her voluptuous skin tantalized. Like sparklers in an ocean breeze, his tingling fingers flared against her breasts, and soon he was sucking each as if they were soft ice cream. Patiently he inched lower, licking her stomach, then along the insides of her thighs, and gently to the marrow of her passion. He nuzzled it and the fluffy hair surrounding it, his tongue thrusting and beating and dallying along her satiny insides. Clutching Tim's scalp Maureen's cries ignited him. He parted her shapely legs. Surely he would quench her. Slowly he penetrated, kissing her and whispering his passion. Gradually the pace swelled: fierce breakers hurling them to ecstasy. Their bodies were in perfect rhythm, their flesh, rocking and swaying in flawless motion as the coach drifted through the night. It seemed the summit of Tim's life. On they surged, hotter they burned until he roared.

"Uh huh," she nodded languidly.

Into her Tim fired a cobra burst. When he glimpsed her eyes they were closed, and from an unmistakable purring he knew she had nodded off.

"But how?" he whispered, quivering in disbelief—his joy shattered, dazed as he wondered whether to confront her.

Maureen woke and motioned how incredible it was. With mixed emotions Tim asked if she was sure she didn't want more. She said that she was happy just to have him in her arms for the rest of the ride. Steeped with disillusion he remained silent.

That date was their most memorable: it would be their last. Maybe Tim should have watched her closely—college consumed much of his time. He loved Maureen as much as he'd ever loved a woman, maybe more, and so when the news hit, he was devastated. He should have sensed the inevitable change, but he didn't realize how deeply she was involved. He knew she never received true recognition for her artistic talent. Maybe she couldn't live with that, or maybe it was just her creative, overindulgent, meditative self.

Tim received a call from Maureen's father who told him to get to the hospital immediately! Maureen was on life-support, but it was useless: thirty-six hours and no change. They'd have to bid farewell. Tim had no idea she was using heroin. She must have been fixing part-time. He hadn't noticed any bruises or spike marks, though junkies tap special places. Mr. Rhodes told him that during the winter Maureen returned from Haight-Ashbury her mother discovered stash and needles in one of Maureen's jackets. They slapped her plenty, but it didn't help. Then they tried the soft approach. Eventually Mr. Rhodes believed she had kicked the habit. That was about the time Tim started dating her.

She was at a friend's the night she overdosed. They must have been partying as usual, only they didn't realize the potency of the dose. Maureen's girlfriend waited for Maureen to get off, and when she saw Maureen's reaction, she decided trying a smaller amount. Minutes later she phoned Maureen's parents, frantic that she couldn't wake their daughter. She wouldn't be specific. Mr. Rhodes raced over and, after smacking Maureen's friend, received a plausible answer. He rushed his daughter to the nearest ER.

Tim arrived at the hospital and nodded dismally at Maureen's brother whose tears and beet-red face confirmed the depth of his sorrow. After a brief hug Brian gestured to where she lay on life-support.

Transfixed by her daughter's stillness, Mrs. Rhodes' eyes were swollen to a pathetic glaze. Her husband dismally paced the room. His beady pupils strained for anything that would make him believe that this was just a bad dream. He settled beside his wife and let Tim pay his last respects. Kissing one of Maureen's cool hands, Tim knelt and gazed at her. This time she was out permanently. She would never again savor life. His face pulsated; his heart surged.

"Maureen, I love you, damn it, wake up—please!" He pleaded. "I'll do anything, get you anything, only look at me—speak to me!" He tapped her cheek . . . no sound, no movement.

Mr. Rhodes brushed his knuckles against Tim's chin. "We decided to take her off life-support. She just wasn't making any progress. God rest her soul."

Tim winced striving to comprehend Maureen as he'd struggled so often with reality. How many times had people seemed fresh and innocent only to be warped or riddled with decay? And why? To Tim Maureen was beautiful, simple, and kind, an innocent daydreamer—he wanted her that way. Yet he realized she was like so many: a pathetic slave to her neurotic pleasures. Though wasn't that the way of the world? How many millions of seemingly innocent souls were either misguided or rotten to the core? How many were compelled by conformity to mask their evil natures?

Tim collapsed into Mr. Rhodes and wept. For the next three months he was severely depressed. If only he was with her the night she overdosed, he could have saved her! Eventually he would have convinced her to quit, or at least cut back. Tim brooded over the possibility of a serious relationship had she lived.

Chapter 10

From April through June Tim was hammered with work. He had to cancel most of his seminars. All of July his partner was away beefing up business in numerous cities. Time flew—August and September vanished.

Early Friday afternoon, the day of his flight, Tim was rummaging through a stack of old appraisal reports for a few samples that might aid his students in D.C. Drifting from the mess on his desk, he envisioned Sheri. Their fateful talk made Tim homesick for his past. He ached for her voice. Even though Sheri had married a complete stranger, he couldn't alienate or deny carrying a torch for her. Yanking the receiver, his taut fingers thumped the keys. On the third ring Sheri's husband answered. Tim was kidding Dan about how great married life must be . . . Dan's bleak response stifled the moment:

"I honestly don't know. She's been missing since yesterday."

Tim's scalp tingled. A whiff of sorrow whistled through him as Dan continued.

"Sheri was with her best friend, Dana, who told me that after they left the mall she dropped Sheri at the mailbox a block from our house. Sheri needed to post a few bills that were overdue. Dana had offered to drive her home; but Sheri insisted that it was so nice out, she'd rather walk. That's the last anyone's heard. I reported it to the police. I combed the neighborhood repeatedly. I contacted everyone we know. I don't know what to do—I'm worried sick! You haven't seen her, have you?" Dan pleaded as if his heart were crumbling.

"No—God, I hope she's all right."

"So do I; I can't imagine being without her the rest of my life."

"Dan, I'm leaving tonight on business. I'll be back Sunday. If I think of anything that might help, I'll call you." Dumbfounded, Tim winced.

Beyond the window pitch dark eclipsed all but a few aircraft lights while in the cabin the faint glow revealed tired travelers. As the jet soared east Tim strived to believe that Sheri was safe. Dan would find her—Dan had to. If he didn't, Tim wouldn't hesitate.

Glimpsing Reagan Airport's towering alloy ceilings speckled with ornate glass domes that shimmered like choice diamonds set in sterling silver, Tim paced to his rent-a-car. Inevitably he strode across cream-colored marble to the front desk of D.C.'s Grand Hyatt. At the base of the lofty atrium, beneath a suspended Stars and Stripes, Tim checked in. Escalators descended, amidst waterfalls and exotic plants, to lounges, restaurants, and a sparkling lagoon. Tim's suite was as agreeable as the rest of the hotel. After wolfing down a BLT he popped on the DO NOT DISTURB tag and retired.

The next morning he felt somewhat refreshed . . . no bizarre dreams he could recall had tainted his sleep. Tim savored a late breakfast before heading to the Burnham Room, which was arranged for an informal class. Something about "Burnham" was disorienting. Visions of booze, bars, and benders flitted through his head—and then he knew: Don Burnham—of course! The alcoholic writer played by Ray Milland in the 1945 Academy Award winner, *The Lost Weekend*. No wonder Tim felt tipsy.

The four-hour session on Motel/Hotel Valuation was typical; not many questions prolonged it; though Tim sensed, from the yawns and weary faces of some of his students, that his offbeat humor wasn't priming interest in the subject. By late afternoon class ended; and as Tim crammed his files into an overstuffed satchel, Sheri's wispy visage pulsated. He raced to a dimly lit alcove and phoned hopeful she'd pick up, but the answering machine bellowed. It was Dan rattling off a standard greeting . . . then he added:

"If this is Mom—I'm doing my damnedest to find Sheri. Please don't worry. I won't give up. I love you, Mom."

"Pick up!" Tim blared. "I'll be back tomorrow. Dan, if you need me, call me—please! I pray you find her." Tim kicked the wall. "Damn!" He was sure Sheri would be home. Dan's message obliterated Tim's optimism. He phoned that night, but no luck.

Tim spent most of the next morning and afternoon reviewing appraisals that were quickly becoming overdue. Seconds before departing he called and got Dan's answering machine. During the flight Tim napped, and at 7 p.m. Pacific time they landed. Ecstatic to be back he bolted to his car and was soon skimming Seattle's suburbs.

Tim lives off of California Avenue in West Seattle's Admiral District, a neighborhood of young aggressive professionals and old-and-faded elite. The houses date from the 1940s to the present; the architecture, a vibrant potpourri of styles.

Years ago Tim purchased a roomy Cape Cod: a reminder of his childhood home in Seminary Valley—the spitting image of that house, only larger. Perched on a small bluff, it overlooks Puget Sound to the northwest, Elliot Bay to the northeast, and, across the bay, downtown Seattle. The view, especially at night with the glimmer of city lights, is breathtaking—almost as breathtaking as the price he paid for it.

Swerving onto his street he cocked his head and marveled at the indigo night replete with gleaming stars. Up the crescent-shaped driveway and into the garage he roared hoping that by the time he reached the kitchen and phoned, Dan would answer. "Busy—damn it!"

Most of the mail was junk, nothing exciting. He strolled to the fridge for something sweet . . . not there, better look up top. Tim spied an unopened pint of Ben & Jerry's New York Super Fudge Chunk. Yanking it out he thought: that's odd, I know had a pint of vanilla sitting next to it. He rechecked the freezer—frozen lasagna, chicken dinners, and ice, but no vanilla. Tim gorged as he contemplated the missing pint . . . then he realized that Dan might have left him a message. His spoon clattered against the oak floor.

From his nightstand the digit 1 glowed. He was optimistic until the recorded voice slithered out: low, guttural, and eerie:

"Howdy." The tone was mocking. "I'm here, and it didn't take me half as long as I figured; neither did the business I attended to, but that's over. However, I do have room for one more—you can be sure of that. I'll be seeing you soon. Until we meet, fatal dreams." His last words were a raspy whisper.

Tim shivered. Though it had been ages since he heard the voice—no doubt it had changed over the years—Tim was convinced it was Robert. To quell his trepidation he rationalized that it wasn't Robert. At least he'd be able to get to sleep. "It's probably a wrong number or a crank call: some bored, frustrated teenager, that's it." Sheri's sullen eyes emerged.

The smoke from Tim's lips floated out the open window. Straining to empty his mind, he eased his pipe into the ashtray. The hall light remained on, just an old habit. Clicking off the reading lamp, he closed his eyes and drifted to his dreams . . .

The crystal moon mesmerized. The landscape was dazzling. It felt like early September, an Indian summer night with a slightly cool breeze—perfect! Back and forth he rocked before getting his seating. Then he settled in for a long ride. The wind lightly lashed his face and chest as he soared over hill and vale atop cantering hoofs. His horse, Neptune, was jet black from nose to tail; a strong, powerful steed who would heed Tim's commands.

Dressed as Washington Irving might have preferred, Tim's long, silky hair was drawn in a snug but stylish queue. A dark, stately cloak flapped against his frock coat, brocaded weskit, and breeches. A ruffled silk shirt, cravat, and clocked stockings complimented Tim's build. Brass-buckled shoes and a charcoal tricorn edged in snow-white ermine completed the image.

He could tell—from the flicker of oil lamps and pierced tin lanterns, and by the olden shops, taverns, and homes he passed, then back to dirt trails with split-rail or stone fences—that he was in post-Colonial times some ten to forty years after the American Revolution, as his mind would have it, bolting from town to town across a primitive Connecticut countryside. The engraved signpost beside the clockmaker's shop at the last borough read:

Bristol Conn
Est 1727

A small roadside inn 15 miles west stoked his curiosity with illusions of unbridled conviviality. A lady had written to him to meet her there to discuss a matter of paramount importance.

There was a hint of flirtatiousness in her words. The letter was signed:

I am, and remain, a most affectionate, and
A Dear Friend.

He was unsure of her identity; nevertheless his heart surged as he whisked across the pristine landscape to meet her. Lush woods parted by soft fields, the moon at his back, and the faint glimmer of the last haven he had passed where most shopkeepers had settled business and many townsfolk had extinguished their candles for a much needed rest: all this and more paraded through his soul. He could care less about sleep. Tim was ecstatic, not only by the prospect of an amorous welcome from a beautiful lady, but that he was riding with ease on an incredible stallion, so close in time to the birth of American freedom, in a land so far removed from present times.

Streaking over steep hills and through velvety glades with radiant brooks, he roared with laughter until, at the crest of a lofty bluff, he spotted the faint luminescence that glimmered like pirate treasure. He knew this was his destination, yet he lingered enamored by the moonlight view. Neptune relished the pure night air while Tim lit a bowl of rum-soaked tobacco. Never had the smoke tasted as savory or the night felt as robust and exhilarating as it was at that very moment. He tapped the briar firmly against the heel of his shoe. Its ashes tumbled to the ginger colored earth. Stowing his pipe he motioned to his steed and bolted into the valley. Neptune escorted him clickety-clack over the cobblestone walk that meandered to the front of the greystone inn. Tim hitched his beauty to a cast-iron post near a trough into which Neptune swiftly thrust his head and lapped the cool water. Tim started to knock when instinct suggested he enter—but not yet . . . the gleam from a distinct fixture charmed his senses: a heart shaped silver-plated door knocker. Soft moonbeams illuminated it rousing a surreal, phosphorescent glow. The inscription on the knocker gently murmured, "*Fatal Dreams.*" Something about the words and fixture, some vague recollection, sparked apprehension. He tried to recall, but the feeling vanished and he was all smiles. Sipping the velvety air, Tim gazed longingly at the resplendent landscape and, with a whisper of a squeak, he entered the inn. A mystic radiance enveloped him: one that penetrated deeper than the genial blaze from the two stone hearths.

The center hallway ambled to a flight of stairs that ascended to darkness. Beyond the hall a bar and check-in appeared, and beyond that, a cookery. In the parlors to his left, Tim noticed a few seated travelers. To his right there was no one. The proprietor was absent; and since there wasn't a soul to greet him, he entered the vacant room and sat by the fire. The walls were adorned with small arms, muskets, braces of sabers, long-stem clay pipes, and tankards and flagons of pewter, leather, and tin, all interspersed with curious engravings of noblemen. As far as he could recall, he had never visited the inn; yet from the depths of his heart enchantment resounded. Out of thin air a decanter of ruby port and two elegant quartz glasses glistened. The nearest glass was replete, as if someone had read his thoughts. Tim stooped and whiffed. The fragrance was so delightful he almost nodded off. Raising the fiery crystal to his lips, he reeled back and marveled at the flavor, his soul aglow with contentment. As he ogled the fire, a woman's voice—as soft and sweet as the intoxicating dram he was savoring—beckoned. It couldn't be, yet there was no mistake. He rushed to embrace this ravishing beauty. No longer a child, her emerald eyes and lush green frock scintillated. Soft auburn locks graced her delicate shoulders and silky back. Against her vibrant skin lay an undergarment of billowy organza chemise. Her smooth, shapely legs were nestled in sheer milk-white stockings with mint-green ribbons fitted slightly above the knee. Rich satin brocade cradled her feet. She was heaven.

"Sheri!" Tim's heart flared. "It's been so long."

"Yes." She lit the room with a soul-stirring smile.

He held her gently and they kissed . . . sweet penetrating embrace from a shimmering spirit.

"Let's sit," she whispered. "I have something to tell you, something you need to know."

Tim nodded and beamed. "But here, have some wine."

"Of course," she replied, her voice caressing his heart.

Toasting one another, gazing into each other's eyes, the radiant fire, the enchantment of the inn: if this was a dream, Tim would have to make it last.

"It's happened," she sighed, "so now you must do something for me."

"Happened?"

"I'll tell you in a minute, but first I need your help. I want to—" Her eyes pulsated as if an unforeseen cataclysm loomed.

"Yes?" Tim implored.

"I—" She was fading. "Someone's coming. Wake up and protect yourself, now!"

"Who? Don't leave—please!" Tim cried out, but Sheri was gone. As he clutched the air pleading for her to return, he started to fade. He fought to remain, but it was too late.

The moon was bleak, the stars, gone; clammy air seeped through his veins. Between his legs zigzagged a flustered nag riddled with wrinkles and welts. She valiantly cantered through the foreboding woods, knocking him against rotted branches and trunks. Tim peered at his clothes and gasped: torn and ragged, they were eaten away as if he'd been wearing them for decades. He ached to burst from this morbid illusion, yet he knew all the kicking and screaming wouldn't help. Wiping the sweat from his brow, he glanced over his shoulder. The tangerine glow swelled. He looked ahead and there was the bridge! Like whiffs of mystic aphrodisiac—no, like beetles on the brain—bygone verses resounded throughout the sinister night:

"The fateful bridge whispers to the sly moon, 'Should he reach the other side, there will be no doom.' Haunted by a gallop—it grows loud and louder—look up! Escape the fatal phantom on his manic steed; his fiery orb cocked, upon his boot a pumpkin seed. Shrouded in midnight gloom—always seeking, always feeding—the ghoul of Sleepy Hollow hounds me to an empty tomb."

Robert had recited this when they were kids marching to the willow tree. Was this the catalyst of the charming dream Tim was wrenched from? Why was Tim always gravitating to him?

"You can't escape the Headless Horseman; your neck he'll break, the Headless Horseman; your soul he'll take, the Headless Horseman; Headless Horseman, Headless HOORRRRRSSSEMAAAANNN!"

Like coarse splinters Robert's poetry pierced Tim's bravado, and then he realized: I'm the lanky schoolmaster—heart in throat—on an old, frazzled mare desperately scrambling to the bridge at Sleepy Hollow, fleeing from a headless ghoul.

The steed of Tim's pursuer was so near, its torrid snorts singed the hairs on his neck; and as Tim turned for one last glimpse, he froze. From the baleful gleam of the wide-eyed pumpkin the rider clutched like a tray of roast duck, Tim could see that the horseman wasn't headless. There was no mistaking the smirk, the leer, the insane laugh.

"Why can't I get rid of you? Stop glaring at me!" He was jolted to reality.

Tim's bedroom—pitch black; the light beside him—useless. He leaped from his bed, raced to the hall, and flipped the switch . . . not even a flicker. The front door creaked open. It was so dark, but wait; a fiery glow struck the lower landing. Shivering, Tim retreated to his bedroom. Footsteps, like the ones in a certain nightmare, thumped deliberately. Tim could hear the chuckling. The light ascended the stairs and floated through the hall. It entered the bedroom, jerked Tim's way, and pierced his eyes before crashing to the floor. Someone stooped to pick it up. Tim cringed . . . The surgeon's gown was equipped with bloody weapons. Elastic fingers gripped a sharp axe. And from the grim shadows a voice—identical to the one on his answering machine—pounced:

"All my life I've been waiting. Finally, you're mine. You thought you were slick spying on me in Pittsburgh. That was a year ago. A lot can happen in a year. You can't imagine in your wildest dreams how or why my friends would help me escape, but they did. That's what I call loyalty. None of your friends would do as much."

"Robert!" Tim screamed.

"Well it isn't Bela Lugosi, and it isn't Sheri—I can assure you. So let's see: who could I be?"

"Where is she? What did you do to her?"

"That's for me to know and for you to mourn."

"You were a great friend. Why did you change? Was it your parents?"

"Try telling them that; I'm sure they'd love to hear your voice." He tossed the flashlight on the bed. Its high-powered gleam illuminated Tim's legs.

Contemplating Sheri's fate, Tim trembled as Robert ranted:

"Can't you see? I must destroy those I love. It frees my mind . . . like the creamy taste of vanilla ice cream sliding down my throat. But I'm afraid you'll never understand, and it doesn't matter because your time is up! I'm taking no chances." He cocked the silvery axe. Its blade slit the ceiling.

Pawing frantically for Robert's arms, Tim shrieked: "Robert, don't, please, aaahhhhhhhhh!"

An unknown voice roared—and wham! The crack of a major-league home run. Tim fell to the floor. His mind churned in a nebulous sea. Familiar voices resonated . . .

First, his: "Merrily, yes, oh so merrily, life is what you dream."

Then, Sheri's: "My husband, Dan Davis; we were married in June of '85. It was a small wedding, just immediate family."

Naylor: "I told ya, Bish, R and J stand for Runt and Jerkoff."

John: "They took care of him all right—put him away for good. Guess ya didn't hear . . . he murdered his parents."

Sheri: "You mean the blood bath! One of Robert's cronies informed my best friend months after it happened."

Naylor: "What about the stitches around the mouth?"

John: "You're not really gonna go there and see Robert, are you?"

Cathy: "Be careful. You said that the guy's weird. I don't want my favorite cousin ending up in the obituaries."

Ed: "All I know is that he butchered 'em fiendishly. I think he used an axe, or was it a hatchet? I can't remember for sure, but when the police found the bodies there was blood everywhere. I guess some freaks don't know when to clean house."

John: "One of these days when he feels like it, he'll march out of that place."

Tim: "I do hope Sheri's okay . . . she should be."

Robert: "Nothing, nothing's wrong, you see; and what could be wrong? Nothing, nothing with me."

The killer in Robert's dream: "But it's your turn. I've made frozen food out of your friends. Now I'm going to make you as sorry as that shrunken head in your pocket."

Tim tried shaking himself awake. He managed to stop the voices, but couldn't reach consciousness. Then he drifted to another dimension too wondrous for words . . .

He and Robert were kids on the streets of their old neighborhood. Beneath the summer sun, in T-shirts and shorts, they skipped barefoot down the sidewalk of Latham Street. Tim was ecstatic.

"Come on," Robert's eyes coruscated, "ya wanna see it, don't you?"

At last! Robert was taking Tim to the hideout. Brimming with anticipation Tim stood beside Robert at the edge of the woods. Robert licked his lips and grinned:

"What a beautiful day—so beautiful, in fact, that there's only one thing that would make it better . . . you know." Robert's temples pulsated.

"Tell me." Tim shrugged.

"Vanilla ice cream."

Without thinking Tim blurted. "I like chocolate."

Robert leered, shoved Tim, and tore into the woods. Tim raced after him and skidded to a stop. From the corner of his eye, like the spider to the fly, Robert motioned to him. Tim rushed over; but when he arrived Robert had vanished. The opening of a cave appeared. The light from inside shimmered like a mound of doubloons. Into the hollow he marched—a zombie to the sugar fields—until the rumble of a giant boulder being rolled into place shook the earth and stopped. Tim was trapped.

"Robert, let me out!" He pleaded. Tim had found the hideout, but at what price? As he realized the severity of Robert's revenge, a manic voice pierced the air:

"You've always wanted to see my hiding place, and with it, my secrets. Now that you're here I couldn't let you leave without getting your fill. Maybe your eyes are stronger than your guts; we'll soon find out. Here's to your curiosity. Let it yank you screaming to your grave!"

The rear of the cave dissolved unearthing the remains of Mr. and Mrs. Bowden, a few unrecognizable skeletons, and Sheri's corpse. Bracing himself Tim cringed. From the muck the putrid cadavers bolted, grabbed him, and started eating him. Tim screamed, punching and kicking until everything dissolved . . .

Alone he floated in darkness, which gradually lifted. A starry image appeared. Tim recognized the eyes. She smiled as if an unfathomable burden had been vanquished. He shouted from the depths. Her maternal voice penetrated his illusions:

"It's finally over. I can leave—be at peace." There was a moment of pensive silence. "You've always meant the world to me. And now you've made it through; you're all right; you didn't die."

"What do you mean? What happened to you? Where are you?"

"Everything will be fine. Just tell Dan I'll be waiting." She peered wistfully through Tim, and, in an ethereal tone that underscored his most intimate desires, she whispered: "There is someone in your future, don't worry. You have so much to look forward to, someone to share happiness like Dan and I."

"But I want you! Where are you?" Tim shouted.

She departed.

Chapter 11

Everything was hazy, as if he were whirling in a vat of pumpkin ale. Fighting to reach the surface, images appeared clearer and clearer until finally he broke through.

Rolling over he felt dizzy. His chest throbbed. He propped himself up and tried to move his feet. The room bobbed in glimmering light. The recycled air had the slight scent of ammonia and urine. He rolled his eyes and wondered whether he was dreaming again or someplace new. There was a strange bubbling noise, maybe from an aquarium or faulty toilet; and a grotesque picture, Tim couldn't make out, loomed—from its center, bony hands seemed to be escaping from a witch's kettle. He turned away and was relieved to see a window. Cool fingertips tapped his wrist. Floating with the rest of the room was a captivating vision. The doctor would be there any minute. She asked how he was feeling. It hurt to speak.

"Is it my imagination, or is there a fish tank somewhere?" His voice sounded gargled.

"You mean the Pleur-evac, to help you breathe, there—see?" She pointed to a red-white-and-blue container the size of a large box of Crayola crayons.

"I was beginning to think I was underwater."

"No." She smiled and nodded at the fat tube that linked the machine to his chest.

"What happened?"

"You have a punctured lung." She adjusted his sheets. "The doctor will tell you more."

"What's clipped to my finger?"

"A pulse oximeter, to monitor your oxygen."

"And this?" Tim pointed to the tubes running from his right hand to a small pushbutton device.

"Pain medication. Press here," she motioned, "when you need relief."

"As much as I want?"

"Only at intervals. It lets you know when you're ready for the next dose."

"If I don't use it, do I rack up more doses?"

"No double or triple shots."

He scanned her enticing face and asked if he was dreaming.

"Of course not," she grinned.

Tim scratched his cheek. "Let me see, I'm probably at Harborview."

She nodded.

You don't need health coverage to be admitted to downtown Seattle's Harborview Medical Center. As a result, homeless and transients wind up there. In an emergency, however, rich and poor are accommodated, which makes for an eclectic mix of patients.

As Tim reveled in his enchanting guardian, she was joined by an older gentleman with slicked-back hair and a shiny monocle. He looked like Teddy Roosevelt, the staunch Rough Rider with beady eyes and a furry mustache. Tim chuckled as he pictured the doctor in army khakis and a jungle hat charging up San Juan Hill, waving a sword, and rallying his troops. Tim had always found Teddy amusing. When Tim was growing up, most of the history books had at least one caricature from the early 1900s in which the former US president was portrayed with a titanic head and a munchkin body. Like Babe Ruth, T.R. would be at home plate gripping a hefty stick, eager to swat the evils of the world. Yet in Tim's mind this couldn't top the vision of the screwball from the movie *Arsenic and Old Lace* who believed he was Teddy Roosevelt: the actor looked, spoke, and behaved just as Tim expected Teddy would. Hearing him shout "Splendid!" or "Bully!" was comical, but the real scream was when he headed to his bedroom. Brandishing an imaginary saber, he'd dash up the staircase as if it were San Juan Hill, howl "Charge!" and slam the bedroom door.

The doctor asked how he felt. Tim's response was slurred, as if he'd had a few martinis:

"Not too bad; I just can't get everyone's voice to stop echoing—and the room, with or without you, sways like I'm on a ship."

He listened to Tim's heart and lungs while monitoring the Pleur-evac. Tim commented that his side throbbed and that he felt as winded as a choked chicken. The doctor turned to the nurse and muttered some instructions. If he had shouted "Bully!" or "Charge!" Tim would've exploded in hysterics.

"You seem quite jolly," the doctor leaned in. "What's your secret? I could use a good laugh."

Tim clenched his teeth to stifle a chortle. "I'm sorry; everything seems amusing—must be the medication. I shouldn't laugh, it hurts."

"Yes it's best to remain calm. I'm Dr. Alan Carter. You have a punctured lung. Do you understand?"

Tim nodded and mused . . . he even sounds like Roosevelt, Tim recollected from movies and documentaries.

"The puncture is a result of a chest wound. Apparently you fell on your back and someone with a sharp instrument landed on you. You've been unconscious for hours. Fortunately your skull wasn't fractured."

Tim tried to recall the previous night's events, but it was useless.

"We have you on two IV's: Demerol for the pain, and antibiotics to restore the perforated lung. The combination of the opiate and accident has made you lightheaded. You'll soon be off the Demerol; that will eliminate the feeling of being at sea. As for your hearing, it should improve in the next few hours. You'll be here for a few days while we assess your condition and run the proper tests. You're lucky the wound is relatively minor. Try to relax and we'll make you comfortable. Here's an item you can use immediately." He handed Tim a small device with an accordion-like tube and mouthpiece attached to what looked like miniature gas-station pumps. "You need to expand your lungs, return them to normal. Use this every day; take as many deep breaths as you can in an hour. Expanding your chest will prevent pneumonia. The nurse will instruct you; it's quite easy. But now I must leave—duty calls." He half saluted and vanished.

Tim couldn't stop grinning. He figured, whatever had happened last night, the worst was over. Besides, who could complain with Teddy Roosevelt for a doctor, and a bewitching nurse? He ignored the echoes and pain and asked his guardian her name.

"April."

"And it's October."

"Yep." She jotted a few notes.

"The best two months of the year."

She nodded and had him breathe through his new toy. Tim felt like he was under a mound of NFL players—the pressure was fierce. He had to stop or he would have collapsed. As she waited patiently for him to regain strength, he pondered her: April's voice and manner were oddly familiar. Something in her eyes sparked him. She acted sisterly or perhaps, from the sweet vibes . . . attracted. Tim shook his head and sighed: you've known her for a moment and you're on heavy-duty medication. He tried to speak, but his throat was parched.

"This will help." From the swivel-top storage station she poured him water.

It'd be nice to know her, he glowed and skimmed her eyes. "Why am I here?"

She blinked pensively . . . and as her lips parted, Tim's eardrums fluttered.

"We can answer that," bellowed the solemn intruder.

Handsome and pushing 60, he ambled meticulously into the room as though he were calibrating each step. His limbs were slender, his muscles, loose, his stomach, slightly paunch from years of assiduous investigation. Short, sandy locks glistened above his faded blues: eyes that sorely needed rest. His disposition reflected countless unsolved cases plus those he had resolved at a high price. The unsavory characters and situations inherent in his profession had foisted an air of cynicism and dry wit upon his dubious demeanor. With a slight southern drawl he cocked his head making sure the nurse was listening:

"My name is Burke, Detective Sergeant Don Burke, Seattle P.D. This is my associate, Detective Simmons."

Don's boyish partner, a cordial prankster, sported a black leather jacket and flowery tie.

Ogling April as he would a sizzling T-bone, Burke turned to Tim and smirked. "How'd the amputation go?"

"Wha—"

"You know, the sex-change operation."

"Oh, I get it," Tim smiled, playing along with him. "I changed my mind, told 'em to forget it."

"All kidding aside, we need to discuss what happened last night." He scanned Tim like a top notch jeweler examining a priceless gem.

Tim frowned, perplexed.

"We need a few answers regarding the homicide."

"Murder?" Tim was startled.

"Let me get the doctor." April turned to leave.

"That won't be necessary." Burke cleared his throat. "We spoke with Dr. Carter."

With a whimsical snicker Simmons nudged Burke, "Yeah, the eccentric with the monocle."

"Can it!" Burke pointed at his associate.

Amused by Simmons flippant perspective, but refraining from offending April, Tim pursed his lips.

April frowned. "The patient broke consciousness an hour ago. He's weak and needs rest, so please be brief."

"Not a problem," Burke cracked his knuckles, "as soon as you leave."

Ignoring the detectives she focused on Tim. "I have some paperwork and patients, but I'll return."

As she headed out Tim glimpsed the ceiling doing his best Jackie Gleason impression and ardently whispered, "How sweet it is!"

"Hmm?" Burke blinked as April's hips departed from his straying pupils.

"Nothing you're man enough to cure."

"Don't be a smart-ass."

"So you're here to discuss what occurred in connection with a homicide."

"Close enough," Simmons snorted.

"Has anyone other than hospital staff visited? Has anyone explained what happened?" Burke squinted.

Tim shook his head.

"Do you know who tried to murder you?"

Tim cringed. "I know who was wielding the axe before I passed out—Robert."

"Robert Bowden? Someone familiar?"

"An old friend. Then I wasn't dreaming. He really was trying to—"

"All sources indicate that to be the case. I almost forgot." Burke fished in his pockets. "I believe this is yours." He slipped Tim a small, shiny object.

Flipping it over Tim attempted to focus on it. "This looks like my house key."

"It fits your front door perfectly," Simmons quipped.

"But mine's with my other keys. This must be the spare I keep under the door mat. What are you doing with it?"

"We found it on Robert's corpse." Burke licked his lips.

"Robert's dead?"

Simmons winked. "He's not in Toledo with Elvis."

"Do you mind?" Burke glared at his associate.

The detective sergeant stated the facts while Tim obsessed over Robert . . . *So Robert had my spare key. How often had he been in my home before he tried to kill me, and what personal effects had he taken or destroyed?* Tim pictured from the sanitarium Robert's grim eyes, and he imagined the uncanny chant that seeped like black juju from his lips:

"Nothing, nothing's wrong, you see; and what could be wrong? Nothing, nothing with me."

Shaking off the uninvited chill, Tim peered at Burke who was pinching his lip.

"Do you know who saved your life?"

Tim shrugged.

"The assailant didn't have heart failure and keel over on you while he was trying to murder you." Simmons' eyes flared.

Burke elbowed his partner. "The same person who gave us your house key—Dan Davis."

"Sheri's husband. Last night I tried to contact him."

"That's another thing: although you seem relieved about Robert's death, which you have every right to be, I have sad news."

Tim realized to whom Burke was referring. "Not Sheri." He prayed the detective would shake his head.

"We're sorry." Burke frowned at Simmons.

Tears formed as Tim struggled to cap his anguish. From past to present, every moment he and Sheri shared rippled through him as if he were on his deathbed; yet he cooperated with the detectives knowing that as soon as they left he would be free to contemplate this pitiful tragedy.

Their verification of Robert's criminal history per Pittsburgh police and regional law-enforcement databases coincided with Dan and Tim's statements. Realizing Bowden's wacko nature— the method by which he murdered his parents and, in all probability, Dan's wife—plus the fact that Dan in slaying Robert saved Tim's life, Burke felt justified that he had released Dan on his own recognizance.

"Yes, the way the investigation is shaping up, it appears Mr. Davis did the right thing. Bowden's death seems like total justice. It would be hard to convict anyone who had acted as Dan had, wouldn't you agree?" Burke probed Tim's face making sure Tim wasn't attempting to withhold anything.

"Absolutely, and somehow I'll repay him for saving my life."

"Just being around to help him pick up the pieces, now that his wife's gone, should be sufficient. After we present the case to the King County Prosecutor, I have no doubt he'll rule Robert's murder 'in office—justifiable homicide': in other words, self-defense."

"A welcome relief for Dan," Tim nodded.

"Oh, by the way," Burke snapped his fingers, "Mr. Davis said that he'd see you today or tomorrow." Burke slipped Tim his card. "If anything comes to mind, or if you need our assistance, please call. The slightest detail can prove invaluable."

As the detectives exited, Tim drifted to Sheri and broke down.

At 11:30 Dick Cline, Tim's appraisal partner, phoned pushing to visit. Tim stressed getting the work out. When Dick mentioned a Saturday seminar in D.C. and how, with all the reports due, he wasn't thrilled about going, Tim told him he'd teach it. Dick insisted Tim recuperate, but Tim wouldn't budge.

Some patients were watching TV game shows, which was the last diversion Tim was in the mood for. He huffed on his lung exerciser and nodded to sleep.

An hour later a light tapping clipped his slumber: a delivery of multicolored helium balloons and a get-well card.

"Here ya are." The courier secured the assortment to the head of Tim's bed and pitched him the card. "From your office—enjoy." He smiled and exited.

Gutting the envelope Tim chuckled. The office staff knew his refined taste in art. Mischievous mayhem permeated the card. With a maniacal gawk and blowfish cheeks, Curly tooted a tuba. Moe and Larry had their hands to their ears, listening. The caption:

GET WELL SOON, TWINKLE TOES!
FROM ALL US BLOWHARDS AT THE SHOP.
WE'RE WORKIN' NIGHT AND DAY AND
'ROUND THE TUBA FOR YA—NUK NUK NUK.

Tim savored each greeting until he remembered he'd never again see Sheri. He rolled over and wept. Even if she had married Dan, he ached for her; the memories were too deep. Why had Sheri and Maureen—the women he most cherished, who incited him with a profound appreciation of life and beauty—died? The hereafter couldn't be more unbearable than life's miserable moments, he hoped. Yet he was sure Sheri had found peace. She would want him to share happiness with someone who would eclipse the emptiness of his heart as Dan had done for her. The more Tim dwelled on this positive insight, the more his melancholy lifted until he reached a stable medium.

With a serving of Jell-O April whirled in to remove Tim's IV's and start him on oral medication. She nodded at the balloons and chuckled at the get-well card; yet she was curious why no one other than the detectives had visited. Tim told her that his mother and stepfather were touring London and wouldn't return until Saturday. Then he explained how backlogged the office was.

"Suit yourself," she shrugged, "though if I were you I wouldn't mind a little well-deserved attention from my co-workers, especially if I could get it legitimately."

"I have all the attention I need." He beamed.

"This'll calm you." April handed Tim an antibiotic with a long name and a Percocet to ease the pain.

She was as striking as when they first met. Her radiance made Tim high. Entranced he drifted to Sheri's lifeless image. April sensed his sorrow and asked if he cared to discuss it. With mournful eyes Tim explained that he was weary, though he'd be in better spirits by dawn.

As dusk muddled the view from his window, hospital staff removed Tim's chest tube: Doctor Carter deemed it necessary because Tim's lung was healing at an extraordinary rate. The procedure was torture. Afterwards the doctor rambled on about the peculiarities of wolverines. Though Tim's side throbbed, his spirits were rejuvenated. He chuckled until his cheeks glistened, then nodded off and drifted to his dreams . . .

From the late afternoon sunbeams his hospital room glowed with tranquility. Facing the window, a young woman in dark silk gazed to the heavens as if she were meditating.

"Maureen!" he shouted.

She grinned impishly. Her ebony eyes twinkled.

"God, I miss you," he sighed.

She fell into a trance and began to vanish.

"Please stay!" Tim's eyes watered.

The slender figure who greeted him was as he imagined in his Colonial dream: dressed in a glamorous gown, her ears adorned with fiery emeralds—undeniably captivating. She blew him a kiss.

"Sheri," his heart foamed, "tell me I'm not dreaming."

She turned to the window, then to him—not as Sheri, but as his angel of mercy who was ravishing.

"I want to tell you how I feel." April blushed, her eyes brimming with passion.

"Yes!" Tim leaned forward with outstretched arms.

Like an Olympic skater in slow motion, April's sleek body whirled.

"No!" Tim laughed.

Attired in century-old U.S. Calvary regalia, Dr. Carter wielded a saber:

"Men, we must do our duty. The enemy is near. The time to act is now!" He clicked his heels, parried his blade, and screamed: "Chaaaarrrrrrge!"

Howling, Tim buried his face. Tears drenched his pillowcase.

Eventually he turned to the doctor, but it was Bish—and Tim was at the Hammond cafeteria.

"Look, kid!" Bish clutched the prune-faced remnant by its hair and offered it to Tim. "A severed head . . . ya want it? I'll sell it to you cheap."

Tim shuddered at the sagging stitches around the mouth. When he turned away, the cafeteria evaporated. He was home in bed, and out his window twilight swirled dismally. Burke shook his finger and leered:

"I wouldn't go anywhere or make any plans. A murder's a murder any way you slice and stack it. I'll be watching you—you can be sure of that."

"What?" Tim glared.

Burke turned and gazed out the window into the night. Transfixed by the flicker from an ornate candle, Tim wondered what had happened to his bedside lamp. He glanced at Burke and was jolted.

"You only thought you killed me." Robert glowered. "You should know fiends like me never die. I'll haunt you forever. You'll never get rid of me, never!"

"Sonofabitch! Tim screamed. "Leave or pay hell when I die."

Robert's image faded, and the ceiling dissolved to a starry sky. Tim's jaw fluttered; his body rumbled. Ready for takeoff he braced himself. With a thunderous blast he soared into the vast night. Higher he jetted through layers of the atmosphere, then into space, his feet propelling him like retro-rockets. Tim marveled at the earth, its image more breathtaking than anything he had ever seen. He peered ahead, and from the deep space the darkness lifted. He knew he was destined for fire! Shuddering in terror he was helpless. The globe's brilliance was so encompassing, he covered his eyes fearing he'd go blind, but it was useless: he couldn't stop glaring at the sun. Blistering heat seared his flesh. He shrieked as his face peeled away; his body bubbled and burst; his bones disintegrated into the blazing core. He was screaming and shaking when he awoke, his chest drenched with sweat. Stiff fingers gripped his shoulder.

"You had a bad dream. Take some water and get to sleep. I'll be back to see that you are in 20 minutes."

He focused on the towering, manly shape. "You're not April."

"She works days." The middle-aged intruder glared and thrust out a taut hand nearly wrenching Tim's off. "Lois Sharp's the name; nursing's my game." She barked like a drill instructor.

Visibly irritated he mumbled: "Just my luck to wake up from a pain-in-the-ass nightmare and be stuck with a pain-in-the-ass nurse."

"What was that?" She blared, eyeing him like a broken vending machine.

"My nightmare was a pain-in-the-ass curse."

"I don't doubt it." She yanked a pen from behind her ear to make notes, then pointed at Tim. "Make sure you drink some water, then get to sleep."

"Amen!" He exclaimed under his breath.

"Speak clearly so I can understand you." She scowled.

"Thanks again." He nodded as she marched off like a storm trooper. Tim knew he'd be pushing it getting back to sleep, but he couldn't stomach a second encounter, so he forced himself.

Chapter 12

The chirping of baby birds woke him. He spotted the nest in a nearby tree. The pristine sky had no intentions of luring him towards the sun. He shook himself and squinted at the picture that had startled him yesterday. The bony hands rising from a witch's kettle was merely a vase of roses. He laughed as he used the toilet. It was a breeze thanks to Dr. Carter—no chest tube or Pleur-evac; nothing like a little freedom. Settling back in bed his breathing exercises were getting easier.

"How are you? You look a little shaky."

Tim tossed aside his lung exerciser and gazed at the clean-cut stranger in burgundy Dockers whose curly hair was styled to perfection. "Who are—"

"Sheri's husband." He casually waved.

"Oh—Dan." Tim perked up. "I'm still a little out of it."

"You should be. You hit the floor like a truckload."

"Thanks to you I'm alive. I owe you."

Slamming his rump in the nearest chair, Dan pressed his fists to his thighs. "Someone had to stop him."

Tall, husky, and handsome, Dan's rugged face and solemn attitude hinted he had racked up a ton of experience for his age. Sheri mentioned that he was a master electrician. Perhaps he would assist Tim with some home-improvement projects he'd been putting off.

"How are the accommodations?" Dan grabbed a tissue and wiped his brow.

"A far cry from home."

"I'll bet." Dan strained to be cordial, masking his anxiety: grief and frustration would soon erupt. "I met your nurse— April, I believe that's her name—very nice. She told me you'd be home in a day or two, maybe tomorrow."

"Yeah," Tim's eyes flared. "She is sweet. When I get out depends on how fast I heal. They wouldn't want me suing them because I bolted early, then had a relapse."

"Right." Dan's face was swollen as if he'd been weeping for hours.

"I'm glad you stopped by. The detectives told me Sheri . . . I'm so sorry. Dan, please . . . tell me how it all happened."

Wincing dismally, Dan nearly burst into tears. He caught his breath, forced a straight face, shrugged, and leered suspiciously at Tim.

"Sheri mentioned you two were childhood sweethearts."

"Yep, though Robert liked to hang around."

"Bastard!" Dan stomped the floor.

Tim nodded. "I totally agree."

"Well," Dan massaged his eyes and sighed. "Thursday evening, the night she disappeared, I contacted everyone I could think of regarding her whereabouts. The next morning I filed a Missing Persons report. By Saturday your message was the only reply. Since there was no news, I thought it best to phone you when you returned from D.C. Some friends I had contacted stopped by. I suggested they call everyone they know and get back to me with all leads. On Sunday morning I was in a panic—why hadn't anyone called? Then I remembered: Saturday night, when I turned the phone ringer off in hopes of getting a decent sleep, I accidentally shut off the answering machine. Exasperated, I flipped everything back on, marched into the den, and slugged down a half a glass of whiskey. I seriously considered drinking myself to death . . . then the phone rang." Dan related the conversation to Tim.

"'Mr. Davis?'

"'Yes.' My voice was slurred.

"'I'm Detective Don Burke, Seattle Police. I need you to come down regarding the Missing Persons report you filed.'

"'What did you find?' My heart was racing.

"'I just need to ask you some questions. There are personal things we need to discuss and I'd prefer to do it in person. Come on down.'

"Burke's tone choked me with angst. 'Sheri's dead—that's it!' I screamed.

"'Mr. Davis.'

"'Dan.'

"'All right, Dan.' He said it very businesslike. 'We haven't confirmed anything, but I do need you to come down as soon as possible. Oh and please do me a favor. Bring any photographs you may have of your wife.'

"'Tell me she's dead!'

"'We don't know. Just bring whatever pictures you have and come down now.'

"I started to cry. I had prayed a miracle would bring her home, but intuition hinted I'd never see her again.

"'Dan, pull yourself together and come down as soon as possible. I'm on the floor where you filed the Missing Persons report. Remember how to get here?'

"'Yes, but I thought you were with Missing Persons.'

"'We often work hand in hand. I'm with Homicide.'

"I dropped the phone, snatched Sheri's photos, and dashed to my car."

Forlorn, Dan scooted his chair closer to Tim who was misty eyed.

"I skidded into the lot at police headquarters and scrambled to the fifth floor. After handing Burke the photos, he pulled out the report.

"'I won't beat around the bush.' He spoke softly. 'I'm sorry . . . your wife has been confirmed as the murder victim.'

"'But how?' I pleaded, desperate for the past.

"'We matched her dental records with records of the decedent. Missing Persons supplied me the information you handed them on Friday, but I was still waiting for the lab results. Minutes before you arrived I knew.'

"I wanted to scream. I wanted to pulverize someone. I wanted so badly for Burke to be a liar. I knew I'd have the rest of my life to mourn, so I shook my head and sucked up my grief. Hold out until you get the complete rundown on Sheri and leave Burke's office, then, anything goes.

"Burke was sympathetic. 'I'm sorry, Dan. Is there anything I can do? Do you want to take a break?'

"'Tell me exactly how she died.'

"'Wouldn't you rather wait until you've had time to sort things out?'

"'Damn it—no!' I leered.

"Burke gazed at his desk. 'The initial cause of death was strangulation.'

"'And after that?' I winced.

"'Why does it matter? The victim was deceased.'

"'What happened next?'

"Burke bit his lower lip . . . 'mutilation.'

"Counting backwards from 100, I bit my knuckles and shut my eyes. At 93 I glared at Burke. He remained silent hoping I wouldn't explode."

Tim fought the urge to cry. "That's horrible. Are you sure you want to continue?"

Dan ignored him.

"'Who killed her?' I barked.

"'We don't know. I was hoping you'd give us a lead.'

"My heart shook. I bolted from my seat and roared. 'I want to see her, now! I don't care what she looks like; she's my wife. I love her—just to look at her one last time, something I can remember.'

"'No you don't.'

"Burke knew that the stigma and trauma I might impose on myself after seeing Sheri in such an appalling condition could last a lifetime. That was something he'd feel directly responsible for if he didn't try everything in his power to prevent it.

"'Believe me,' he urged, 'she's in no condition to view. That's not the last memory you want of your loved one. You'll eventually assume possession of her. Wait until the funeral home has her looking decent, then see her—trust me.'

"I capped my hysteria and yielded to Burke's logic. However, the minute the mortician had her presentable, I'd see her.

"I was in dire need of a smoke. Burke escorted me to daylight. The wind and sun were a relief, but the cigarette hit the spot. Back in Burke's cubicle his partner, Simmons, joined us. Burke asked if I had an inkling who the perpetrator was. I couldn't think of a soul or clue. That was before I found Sheri's diary."

"Diary?" Tim's ears perked.

"I'll get to that later. This is hard, but— well—"

Dan's anxiety was obvious. What was agonizing to him was just as unbearable for Tim. Neither of them wanted to acknowledge the tragedy.

"I pried a blow-by-blow description from Burke so that in my mind there'd be no doubt what had happened to her:

"Early Sunday morning a dispatcher from 911 received an urgent call from the Freemont City Transfer Station. One of their trash-truck drivers while unloading some refuse caught sight of an unusually shiny object. He thought it might be something valuable someone had accidentally tossed out. It was the gold bracelet I gave Sheri three years ago on her birthday. As the driver snatched it, something he glimpsed sent him screaming to his boss. Mixed with the debris was Sheri's remains; portions had spilled from a loosely tied sack. As he stared in disbelief he noticed rips in the sack and a half-gnawed leg—rats had started to feed."

Tim bit his thumbnail and quivered.

"Police arrived followed by Burke and Simmons. The detectives pried Sheri's remains from the garbage. Her head, swollen the size of a pumpkin, was crawling with maggots. Burke was disgusted. Simmons excused himself. Two additional detectives handled the crime scene while Burke and Simmons questioned the driver and his supervisor. Back at headquarters they cross-referenced their findings with Missing Persons, and after examining my report Burke contacted me."

Tim ran his fingers through his hair. "How did it happen?"

"I'm coming to that . . . When I last saw Sheri she had the day off from counseling and was headed to the mall with Dana, a close friend. I left work for home around noon to have lunch. Sheri was clutching a stack of bills to be mailed, gazing out the living room window, deeply disturbed. When I asked her what was wrong, she told me we'd discuss it at dinner;

then she pecked me on the cheek and flew out the door. Dana called that night and was surprised when I told her Sheri wasn't home. Dana had dropped her off at the mailbox a block from our house." Dan shook his head. "Burke believed—after he discovered Robert's corpse and uncovered the misdeeds from his sordid past—that the mailbox was the last thing Sheri saw. He speculated that Robert had been stalking her, waiting for the right moment to catch her alone. Well he forced her away, strangled her, mutilated her, stuffed her in a sack, and dropped her at the local dump—Sonofabitch!" Dan clenched his teeth. "Sheri used to mention how Robert mooned over her. I guess through the years the scumbag carried a perverted torch for her. Burke said that committing rape was typical for someone with Robert's personality; yet the crime lab reported no semen on or in Sheri or on her clothes—thank God. Maybe when he attempted to rape her, she said something to piss him off and he strangled her, I don't know." Dan hung his head.

Strangling Sheri seemed contrary to Robert's standard MO. In addition to the method by which he disposed of his parents, to Tim's recollection, the killers in Robert's childhood tales never choked their victims: they preferred axes or knives. Yet Dan's comment about Sheri ticking Robert off made sense. She took crap from no one—one of her qualities Tim had always admired.

Dan glanced drearily around the room and whispered, "I can't get over the shock."

Tim sighed. "It's incredible how screwed up Robert became. If anyone were to tell me that one of my childhood playmates would murder his parents and another of my childhood play-mates, I'd have said that Robert was bizarre, but I couldn't con-ceive he'd have enough hate or insanity to do it."

"Well now you know different!" Dan snapped.

In the distance Tim glimpsed a pair of angel eyes and a quiet smile waiting patiently. "April," his heart shimmered.

Like fresh jasmine her voice graced the air. "I wanted to make sure you finished talking. I'm here to check your tempera-ture and give you medication."

Tim smiled. "Sure, oh," he gestured with an upturned palm to Dan, "I believe you've met, but I'll introduce you. Dan Davis, this is April, the phenomenal nurse who's taking care of me."

"Hi again." Dan nodded.

"It's nice you came to visit." She slid a thermometer between Tim's lips and turned to Dan. "You'd be surprised how many people don't. I'm sure he appreciates your company." She smiled politely.

"I guess so, under the circumstances."

"That's something I'll leave the two of you to discuss," April plucked the thermometer from Tim's mouth, "as soon as I'm finished."

"Appreciate it." Dan straightened his belt.

April glimpsed the glowing digits. "Temperature's not bad." She watched Tim swallow his pill, then asked about his lung exercises. Tim blew a few breaths and she was impressed.

Tim gazed mischievously at her. "I was about to tell Dan that the night service is a far cry from the care you get during the day."

"How's that?" April cocked her head.

"The night nurse, Lois, or whoever she is, can't hold a candle to you."

"You mean Lois Sharp? She *can* act a bit clinical."

"Sharp she may be, but understanding like you, she's not."

April eyes met Tim's, and for a split second she was transfixed. She blushed and turned away. "I won't keep you from your company. Call me if you need me."

Tim smiled. "I'll make it a habit."

April shook her head and exited.

Tim turned to Dan. "Is she sweet?"

Dan nodded.

"Remind you of anyone?"

He glared at Tim. "You don't mean Sheri."

"Who else?" Tim realized his blunder. His mind was muddled; must be the medication.

Dan jumped up and screamed: "Why the fuck would you ask me that at a time like this?! What the hell is the matter with you—asshole?!"

"Dan, I didn't—"

"Sheri's dead, and all you can think of is how she reminds you of a nurse you have the hots for?"

"But Dan—"

"Tell me, dickbrain, how you really felt about my wife; go on, please, so I can punch you so hard you'll never wake up. Come on, fuckwad, tell me you didn't have an affair with Sheri! I swear if you were well enough I'd lay you out cold." Dan shook his fist.

Tim quickly collected his thoughts. "You're right, I screwed up. I shouldn't have said it. I'm sorry. Please accept my apology. I had no right to—"

"Screw you!" Dan shook his head and began to weep.

Tim realized not only the extent of his mistake, but how intensely Dan loved Sheri. "I swear I didn't mean to upset you. Let me say, because you need to know: Sheri and I never had anything more than a childhood friendship. Sure we cared about one another when we were kids; but on my honor it never went beyond that. I never saw her as an adult, before she—the tragedy. I guess when I blurted out that April looked like Sheri, I was too blind to realize how much you cared for Sheri. I really respect you for that, believe me. I screwed up. I'm sorry."

Dan shook his head. "I'm leavin'."

"Wait!"

Dan jerked a Winston from his pocket. "I need a smoke. I may return."

"Dan, please . . . I am sorry."

As Dan darted from the room, Tim realized what had attracted Sheri to him: Dan was handsome, seemingly honest, sensitive, and no-nonsense like Sheri.

Tim pondered Dan's craving for a cigarette—like Maureen and her heroin: if he had only saved her. And Sheri . . . Tim sorely missed her, yet he was sure she had found peace, something most people yearn for, and with that she's bound to be happy. Coming to terms with her death was getting easier. There was no other way but to see it in a positive light. Sheri had been liberated from life's perpetual struggle; and as much as he wanted her in this world, Tim envied her for her newfound freedom. Someday, he was sure they'd meet again.

Dan marched into the room and took his seat.

"How was it?" Tim tapped his lips pretending to take a drag.

"Good enough." Dan frowned.

"Give me a pipe or a fine cigar and I'm set, especially if there's a shot of whiskey or a cold beer to go with it." Tim could see that Dan was anything but amused. "Seriously, I was out of line. I realize how much you miss Sheri. I'm truly sorry. Please finish explaining what happened."

There was silence for nearly a minute. Sheepishly Tim peered at his blanket.

"Don't ever say anything like that again." Dan pointed at him.

Tim nodded with half-closed eyes, slightly in la-la-land from the pain pill.

Chapter 13

" Early Sunday afternoon, after Burke convinced me not to view Sheri, we went over the police report. Simmons, who had just joined us, remained silent. By the time we were through, I felt I had answered a million questions, and all the time, Burke kept eyeing me, double-checking his notes, making sure my answers made sense. He asked if I'd be willing to take a polygraph. I said 'no problem.' Burke suggested searching my home for evidence and clues—anything to nail the killer, but I wasn't in the mood, so we agreed to do it the following day.

"As I left Police Headquarters my thoughts steered me to Mom's. After breaking the news we reminisced about the past and Sheri. When I tried chugging some scotch from her liquor cabinet, Mom was adamant that the only way I'd see things through would be to talk it out: so we did, over a decent supper. Thirty minutes later I was home snoozing to one hell of a nightmare . . .

"I paced the echoey corridor until the familiar letters on the steel-plated door appeared. And in the blink of an eye, I stood dead center in the medical examiner's room—a spacious lab with yawning sinks and goliath scales. The chilled air reeked of human residue and formaldehyde. On a gurney, under a pale sheet, she waited. As I gazed with foaming apprehension, Burke appeared. He acted cold and distant, as if he wanted me to leave the room. The examiner emerged through a side door, and Burke waved. We faced the gurney, our pupils scanning lumpy linen. The examiner gave me an odd look before unveiling the top portion. I urged him on. Slowly he uncovered the head. I gasped when I saw her face: so drained, so white, so alien from the woman I had married. I pictured her body in pieces under the sheet. How I wished to God it was someone else. Screaming in anguish I awoke. It was 8:30 p.m. I started poking into places, searching for her pictures—anything to feel close to her. In a bottom drawer, tucked under old clothes, I found her diary."

Dan jerked a wad of paper from his pocket and pitched Tim the top sheet:

DIARY—I'M OFF WORK TODAY AND FRIDAY—WHAT A RELIEF!—GOING TO THE MALL WITH DANA— ROBERT'S SICK LETTER AND CRAZY POEM ARRIVED— AFRAID HE MIGHT DO SOMETHING—MUST TALK TO DAN TONIGHT!

"Whew!" Tim flinched as he returned the note.

"I was upset after reading that," Dan mournfully glared, "but that's nothing compared to my reaction as I examined Robert's demented poem and letter. They fell out of Sheri's diary as I was thumbing through it. Read this first. The police have the originals."

Gazing at the handwriting, Tim thought it ironic that such a deranged person would write so neatly. As for the content, that was another matter. The poem was addressed, "To Sheri, with love."

THE WINDS OF PAIN

THE WINDS OF PAIN
BLOW THROUGH MY BRAIN
THE SECRETS I CAN'T HIDE
THE LUST I FEEL INSIDE

THE ONES I LOVE WILL FADE AWAY
I MAY NOT LIVE ANOTHER DAY
TO SEE THEM WRITHING IN THEIR GRAVES
ALONE, I HEAR THEM STALKING
I TRICK THEM WHILE THEY'RE TALKING
AND I ESCAPE, I FLY TODAY
TO FIND YOU, LOVE, SO FAR AWAY

THE WINDS OF PAIN
BLOW THROUGH MY BRAIN
THE SECRETS I CAN'T HIDE
THE LUST I FEEL INSIDE

FROM COAST TO COAST I GO
MY STEELY AXE IT GLOWS
INTO YOUR HEART IT FLOWS
YOUR FACE I SEE IT CLEAR
I NEED TO BREATHE YOUR FEAR

THE CRYSTAL NIGHT WHEN I AM DONE
AND YOU MY LOVE NO LONGER COME
I MIGHT TEMPT FATE AND PULL A GUN
TO SHOOT TO KILL

THE WINDS OF PAIN
THAT RACK MY SEETHING BRAIN
THE SECRET I CAN'T HIDE
MY LUST . . . FOR YOU HAVE DIED

"Man!" Tim's eyes bulged. "What makes a person freak like that?"

"There's more—here." Dan exchanged the poem for the letter, which was written in a flowery style.

Dearest Sheri,

I must see you. It's been so long and I miss you so much. You'll never know how much I love you. I always have and always will. I crave every inch of you. I've waited for years to lick the sweat from your skin, and now it's only a matter of days. I hope your heart's beating as fast as mine.

You'll never guess what I've been doing all these years. Oh, but that's right, a mutual buddy forwarded the news about my parents to your best friend. Wasn't that a scream? Ah, but now they're resting in peace. I couldn't have executed it better. You see I loved them so dearly I had to sever them from their misery.

You remember when we were kids, that wild dream I told you and Tim under the willows? You were curious who the killer was. I had to grow up to find out, and growing up spawns revelations. Now that I know, I thought you'd like to. It was I, a grown-up version of me—the adult Robert: he was the killer in the dream. Makes you want to die laughing, doesn't it? I almost did.

I have something else that will put your mind at ease. The night I told my dream, you interrupted me with a story about how you and your girlfriend, Pam, saw a shadow prowling the upstairs bathroom of your parents' house. I wonder who that was—hmm. I remember I visited that night, but you weren't home. That upset me, but I got in anyhow and started my search. I was looking for something of yours I could keep, something that would always remind me of you, and I found it . . . a mound of your hair in the waste basket of the upstairs bathroom. *Pretty clever, huh? Don't worry, I've taken excellent care of it. You remember John, my adorable shrunken head? Well he's still with me and I'm still crazy about him. I rub his rubbery face and stroke his silky hair every chance I get. Only now he has your hair. I couldn't resist. I sewed it on tightly so that I'd never lose it. That was my way of keeping you close all the years you've been away.*

Oh, and don't think I don't know who visited me a year ago. He thought he could fool me, but what he doesn't realize is that I know all and I see all. You can tell Tim that I haven't forgotten him. I intend to pay my last respects.

It's too bad you never visited my secret hiding place, remember? We could have had so much fun there. You would've been amazed at how satisfied I would have made you, but when I asked you, you were never interested. We'll see who's interested when I visit.

And Sheri, remember all the times I used to call you on the phone and tell you all those sweet things? I do. Remember how I used to stand in your backyard watching you comb your hair, waiting for you to come to me? You will come to me. You will be mine. Never forget, Sheri, Sheeeerrrrriiiii!

It wasn't hard finding where you live. As much as I love computers, I didn't use one. The mutual acquaintance who told your best friend about my parents told me about you. That was gracious of him.

But I need you to understand. You'll feel much better after you're gone. I hope you don't hate me for this, but I have to do it. And when I'm finished and you're in beautiful fragments, you'll be happy I did. But why do it? Because everything and everyone I ever loved as a child has to go. I can't live with the memories. And after I've put you and your true-blue Tim in never-never land, I'll be able to bask in eternal glory.

I'll be seeing you soon, perhaps the day you get this letter. Don't forget to save me some vanilla ice cream. I'm lost without it. Until we meet, fatal dreams.

Yours Forever More,

Robert

P.S. The poem is dedicated to you. Read it and cherish it. Let it transform your soul.

Tim shivered as he handed the letter back to Dan. "What a bombshell. I'm surprised Sheri didn't faint after reading it—pure insanity; and Robert: what a maniac."

"I couldn't agree more. That was the icing on the cake. I wanted to kick the living shit out of him, but I guess I went beyond that. Though if anyone deserved it . . . I still can't believe what he did."

Tim nodded as his mind shifted gears. "Something strange that happened the night Robert attacked me is beginning to make sense."

"Yeah?" Dan stowed his papers.

"Vanilla ice cream: Robert's always been partial to it."

"What's strange about that? There are a trillion people who agree with him. Hell, I like vanilla!"

"Let me explain." Tim sipped his water. "When I arrived home the night he attacked me, one of the first things I did was grab some fudge-chunk ice cream from the freezer. The vanilla, which sat next to it, wasn't there."

"So you think Robert was in your house while you were gone and had the ice cream as a snack."

"Yeah, but who knows how many times he visited; though he wasn't there when I arrived Sunday night. He was probably doing something perverted to pass the time, thinking he'd hit my place later and finish business. Burke gave me my spare house-key, which was found on Robert's corpse, so Robert must have been in my home at least once while I was away. That's eerie." Tim stared out the window straining to purge Robert from his mind. "Are you sure he's dead? Did you check him thoroughly? I don't want to worry the rest of my life about getting to sleep."

"Let me put it this way." Dan cracked his knuckles. "The only way Robert could be alive is if Dr. Frankenstein stitched him back together and jolted him with electricity. As far as I know, science hasn't concocted a way to resurrect the dead."

"Stitched him together? What did you do, dissect him?"

"I'm coming to that, if you'll let me continue."

Tim nodded.

"After reading Robert's letter I knew you were in danger. I also realized it'd be my one chance to nail the son-of-a-bitch before he escaped or was arrested. Your address and phone number were on a Post-it note in Sheri's diary. I knew the location of your street because I'd done electrical work there. When I called, your line was busy, so I phoned Burke, explained the situation, told him your address, and said that I'd see him there.

"'Don't leave.' He was gruff. 'If you're concerned, I'll have a unit check it.'

"'With all due respect, I'm going. I'll see you, or whomever you send.'

"'If you must go, please wait for the police. Don't enter before they get there.'

"'I'm outta here—bye.'

"I slammed my car into drive and roared up First Avenue. Zipping through Normandy Park I snagged Route 509 north and swerved off at the White Center exit. I headed to Roxbury Street and through White Center to California Avenue. Cutting off my headlights I pulled quietly into your driveway and dashed across your lawn. Through the pane above your front door, I glimpsed a light ascending the stairs. I poked my head inside and witnessed an anonymous gaunt figure toting a high-powered flashlight; I was sure it was Robert. As he reached the top of the stairs, he chuckled. I swear he sounded like the guy who did the original radio broadcast of *War of the Worlds*."

"Orson Welles?"

"Right. Anyway, I ran to my car, popped the trunk, and grabbed my pride and joy: a number 4 Mickey Mantle Louisville Slugger. I was gonna pulverize that slimeball for what he did to Sheri. I prayed Mickey wouldn't fail. I raced quietly upstairs. His axe was raised, his flashlight, shining your way. He was ready to chop you into steaks. I caught that mother completely by surprise. The second he saw me he screamed and bobbled his weapon. The head of the axe landed flat against his right shoulder; the blade faced his collar. Robert yanked out a dagger, but it was too late. I was already into my swing, wailing at the top of my lungs, 'Here's one for my wife and Mickey you fucking bastard!' The bat slammed the back of the axe head whizzing the blade through Robert's neck like a sickle through marmalade. His head popped across the room and exploded thru the window. With a sickening crunch it landed in the side yard. Grabbing the flashlight I flipped the nearest light switch— nothing. Robert must have cut the power. I aimed the flashlight at the floor, and there he was on top of you. As I rolled his body aside, I noticed a surgical gown tied to his waist with sharp weapons in the pockets—bizarre! Then I spotted a crumpled piece of paper. Before examining it I instinctively poked into his shirt pocket and out came your house key. I thought it was mine—looked just like it—so I pocketed it. It was after I gave it to Burke that he tried it on your front door and it worked. I focused on the crumpled paper. A message scrawled in what looked like dried blood hit me head-on: *FATAL DREAMS*."

The image of the doorknocker at Robert's parents' house and the one at the inn in Tim's Colonial dream flickered in Tim's mind.

"Fatal dreams—yeah!" Dan stomped the floor. "I damn well gave Robert a dose of his fatal dreams. Anyways, I tossed aside the note and surveyed you. There was blood on your chest . . . and beside you—Robert's knife. I tried to wake you, but it was no use, so I used your phone to call for an ambulance. Thank God Robert hadn't severed the phone lines! The police and Burke and Simmons arrived. Police did a sweep of the house, Burke examined you, and Simmons contacted headquarters and the power company while grimacing at Robert's headless corpse and the bloody axe; he shook his head and wisecracked about the surgical gown. The ambulance from Harborview arrived followed by Crime Scene detectives. As medics wheeled you from the house, one of the police officers accompanied you to the hospital." Struggling to control his rage and grief, Dan clenched his fists and whispered: "Crime Scene found, in Robert's back pocket . . . Sheri's driver's license and . . . a pair of her panties. I nearly passed out." Dan closed his eyes briefly, hung his head, and continued. "After questioning me Burke decided not to book me provided I remained in town until the case was settled. I was quick in getting home, though it was hell getting to sleep. That's everything." Dan sighed.

"Incredible!" Tim shook his fists. "And nailing Robert the way you did: unbelievable! As for saving my life, if there's anything you want—"

"Forget it. You know, the one consolation is that it looks like I'm off the hook with Robert's murder. After reviewing the evidence, plus the statements you contributed, Burke—"

"And saving my life."

"Right. Anyway, Burke explained it to the DA and they agreed not to file charges. But murdering someone," Dan popped a Life Savers, "is a terrifying thought. I never imagined I'd do anything half that crazy."

Tim sneered. "Robert was deranged. He committed hateful murders and paid the price."

"I know Sheri and Mickey would be damn proud of that."

"I'm sure they would." Tim beamed.

"Though if I had only nailed Robert sooner, she'd be alive." On the verge of tears Dan pressed his knuckles to his cheeks.

"There's nothing you could have done. But hey," Tim adjusted his pillow. "I recall Robert, before trying to kill me, jabbering something about how he escaped from the state hospital in Pittsburgh."

"Burke didn't tell you?"

"I was out of it when he and Simmons stopped by."

"Well, according to Burke, two of the cooks at the facility were friends of Robert. Robert had a cornucopia of allies. He was awesome on the Internet and one hell of a computer geek. Having buddies who worked at the place was pure luck;

maybe they were friends of friends. Regardless, they knew what he wanted and were more than willing to oblige. I'm sure he promised them the moon. And they weren't the only ones. One of the guards was in on it—he procured security uniforms for Robert and the cooks. Late one night Robert's accomplices slipped the staff sedatives and locked the doors to all the cubicles; this insured that the inmates wouldn't run amuck and hamper the scheme. Robert's part was child's play. Seconds before they locked his cubical, Robert quietly slipped out, donned his uniform, and was escorted to freedom."

"What about the guard on the first floor who oversees the video?"

"With assistance from the corrupt guard, the cooks patched a cable and switchbox apparatus to the security monitor system. The cable ran to a video player tucked in the basement. During the change of shifts, one of the cooks hit the 'play' switch. As the new guard assumed his post, he thought he was viewing everything as normal from the cameras positioned throughout the building, but he was really watching a recording from the previous night."

"I guess if someone needs to escape there's always a way."

"Yeah," Dan smirked, "Robert found a way—to hell, and I hope he's miserable."

Tim nodded. "I still can't get over the letter—you know, where he stated he'd have to kill everyone he ever loved as a child because he couldn't live with the memories. He must have felt that way after murdering his parents."

"I'm sure it predates that. It's crazy how certain premonitions come true: Robert's childhood dream plagued by his future spirit—the lunatic, the pervert, the bastard that wrecked my life, the fucking son-of-a-bitch that killed my wife!" Dan wept.

Tim grabbed a tissue and passed the Kleenex to Dan.

"Robert screwed me." Dan patted his eyes. "Hell, I'm pushing forty, my life's half over, Sheri's gone, and now what?" Dan peered at the ceiling, shell shocked.

Tim snapped his fingers. "Most of your life you've been fortunate. I've always admired Sheri. She was sincere, honest, and giving. Dan, if you hadn't come along I might have married her, then I'd be in your shoes. I wish I had half the time you had just being around her. I know how empty and heartbroken you feel, but you *will* make it."

Dan gazed curiously at Tim. "Are you sure you and Sheri—"

"Never."

"Okay."

"Again, thanks for saving me. Name it: anything you want, anything I can do!"

Dan shrugged. "You know it's sort of nice having someone to talk to, someone my age, someone who can relate to the situation."

"Yep." Tim nodded and pondered . . . Sheri had done alright. He really couldn't fault Dan; besides, where was Tim when she needed someone to lean on? As he pictured Sheri he glanced at Dan who was biting his nails. "What about the funeral?"

"She's being cremated. There'll be a small service. She would have preferred it that way." Dan nodded.

"You *did* see her before she was——"

"Yes, before I came to see you. The mortician did a fine job. Burke was right. I'm glad I waited. I don't think I could've stomached seeing her messed up."

"Just let me know when the service is."

"Friday; and since you'll be out of here in a day or so, you should have no problem making it."

"I'll be there." Tim scratched his chin.

Dan stood up and nodded. "I'm out of here."

"Dan," Tim gazed earnestly, "I can't tell you how sorry I am about Sheri."

"That pain and sorrow I'll bear till I die. I don't believe I'll ever get used to it."

"Dan, if you need someone to talk to, please . . ."

He flipped Tim a card. "Here's the name and address of the funeral home. I'll see you on Friday."

Chapter 14

An hour later reporters stopped by—the main topic was Robert. Tim dished out the ammo: a number of Robert's psychotic quirks plus a few of his grisly stories. After they left, Tim settled back and smiled: he'd probably be released tomorrow. It'd be great to be home. Hell, it'd be great to get out and do things. Sheri's smile flickered rousing bittersweet memories that lulled him to sleep.

Just before dinner Tim woke to a vision of evergreen trees and an azure sky. How brilliant the trees of his old neighborhood would be, still half-dressed in multicolor—a lush autumn cascade that would soon wither to cocoa brown like their dead brothers and sisters who lay shriveled on the faded grass below. Was he spacing out or what? As he turned from the window, April arrived—enchantress. The food was bland, but the service, perfection. Unlike the firm, clinical tone of some staff, April's voice was soft, surreal, wonderfully inviting. Her nails weren't long, but polished to perfection; her skin, smooth and slightly tan; her ruby curls, gleaming; her lips, sensuous and sweet. Yet it's the eyes: the soul of a person's makeup. April's heart soared from her irises. With every glance Tim fought to conceal his desire. Would he feel the same when he was home? From her conversations and interactions with staff, he believed she wasn't in a relationship. "April in October," he whispered, "what a combination."

As she prompted him to eat, Tim recalled . . . there was something inimitable in her style. She conjured up his idyllic childhood graced by someone Tim would forever cherish.

"Well," April's eyes twinkled, "you devoured that. You must be feeling better. Tomorrow you'll be ready to leave."

"Yeah, dinner must have been decent," he kidded, then paused . . . but I wish I didn't have to go."

"How do you mean?"

"I enjoy the service here; but more than that I enjoy the company. Something that fine can be hell to find on the outside, you know?" He probed her eyes . . . what was she thinking?

Welling with disenchantment April glimpsed the floor. "It's been ages since I've really enjoyed myself. I'd like to let go, but I was hurt badly the last time; and when someone shatters your happiness, you lose faith in so many things. You wonder if love is poison. I couldn't stomach what I went through before. If it happened again I'd either end my life or live alone for the rest of it."

Tim nodded. "So often I thought I had it made, but things changed and before I knew it I was heartbroken and alone. Since my last wipeout I've thought long and hard about my future. I'm ready for life, win or lose. After all, nothing ventured, nothing gained. When the time is right and opportunity calls, I won't let it escape; life is too short. I now see that opportunity. I'm ready to open up, to give again. I've never made promises and abandoned them. I'd never do that as surely as I'd never hurt anyone I truly cared about."

April's gaze was penetrating, as if she were reading his soul. Suddenly she blinked, lifted his tray, and headed out, then stopped and turned to him. Tim sensed she was contemplating a momentous decision; this she settled with a grin, and for a brief moment she appeared childlike, undeniably content.

"I have to make my rounds, but I'll be back. Before I forget, most of the staff will be in costume."

"Oh?" Tim shrugged.

"Halloween. Every year we dress up, for fun. It jump starts the patients' spirits."

"My spirit jump starts every time you enter the room."

"I have to go," she smiled, "but I'll return. I have a surprise."

"And you won't tell me?"

"It wouldn't be a surprise." She waved goodbye.

In the vision he had when he was knocked unconscious, Sheri told him not to worry—there would be someone in his future. He'd have to make a date with April. After all, nothing ventured, nothing gained. Love, joy, friendship, and intimacy could eclipse their emptiness. Tim knew she favored him more than just out of kindness. Her voice was so inviting, her smile was so sweet, her eyes brimmed with such understanding, that he'd have to find an excuse to extend his stay.

Later that evening, as Tim practiced his breathing, the commotion paraded past his room. He nodded at their outfits and chuckled at their gregarious chatter. Space aliens, monsters, vampires, devils, witches, and historical celebrities: they seemed to be having a blast.

Halloween has always been Tim's favorite time of year. He longed to be home doling out trick-or-treat candy and scaring the kids.

As Tim reached for his drink, he was blasted against his pillow by a roar that shook the room.

"Tennnntion!" bellowed the voice from the staunch figure that blocked the doorway.

Tim did a double take. It was Dr. Carter dressed in vintage khakis, military boots, and pith helmet. A shiny saber was hooked to his side. Tim wondered: had the doctor been eavesdropping with his stethoscope on Tim's dreams? Tim howled with laughter. This was too good to be true.

Doctor Carter adjusted his monocle and pointed at him. "Don't you know it's army regulations to salute in the presence of an officer and commander-in-chief?"

"Yes, Mr. Roosevelt." Tim saluted and corrected himself. "I mean, yes sir, Mr. President."

"That's more like it."

The doctor marched in, whirled 90 degrees, advanced three paces, and scanned Tim.

"Well . . . how do I look?" he queried as if he were headed to a cabinet meeting.

"Simply splendid Mr. President." Tim grinned.

"That's bully, just bully. Well, I'm off to the front; mustn't disappoint the ranks. Besides, you'll be discharged tomorrow and back to the real world. Life out there is a jungle, you know. I hope we've made your stay comfortable as well as entertaining while you were recuperating."

"Yes Mr. President, by all means, sir."

"You look fit as a fiddle. I hear you've made headway with your breathing. That's commendable young man, simply commendable. Keep up the good work and keep your chin up."

"Yes sir." Tim saluted one last time.

Doctor Carter marched off, but not before halting at the doorway. Struggling not to laugh, he turned to Tim, peered solemnly, and brandished his saber. "Chaaaaarrrge!" he screamed as he bolted from the room.

Tim exploded in hysterics. Maybe the doctor was an escapee from a mental institution.

Recalling the last scene from *The Wizard of Oz* (the consoling farmhands at Dorothy's bedside) Tim wondered who would be next to pay his or her respects—but she had already drifted in: resplendent, in full glory, the eighth wonder of the world! Adorned like Sheri in his Colonial dream, April's luxurious gown and emerald earrings were mesmerizing.

"I called the costume shops until I found one that had the style of dress you mentioned."

"What?" Tim was awestruck.

"I couldn't help overhearing some of the details you referred to while you were sleeping. You must have incredible dreams."

"Not as incredible as you. You're amazing!"

"So are you," she caressed his knuckles.

For a moment April became Sheri; it was inevitable, the way April was dressed. Tim quivered as he pictured his childhood—that first date: biking neck and neck under a blazing sun, Sheri offering him valentine candy, listening shoulder-to-shoulder to their favorite song, imagining being married, and the kiss at the top of their street. Those bewitching memories would forever define him.

Sheri had mentioned becoming a nurse and caring for him when he was sick. Tim gazed at April. Sheri's image vanished. Here was his chance to end the loneliness and broken dreams. Sheri and Maureen had departed; but April . . . he'd be a fool to let her go.

"I must have been talking in my sleep." Tim cleared his throat. "I hope I didn't say anything embarrassing."

"No." She handed him his juice. "A toast," she clacked her bottle of Perrier against his cup, "to dreams."

"Right." Tim felt higher than any experience had ever propelled him. "They can come true . . . if you truly believe in them."

Like two lovers toasting a sumptuous meal, they glowed. Tim realized that what Sheri had expressed to him in a recent dream, about finding true love, seemed inevitable.

Chapter 15

As intensely as he longed to stay with April, Tim needed to return to work. He explained his friendship with Sheri and the details of her tragedy. April was sympathetic, yet Tim sensed she was curious how intimate he and Sheri had become. Tim told April he'd call her as soon as he returned from D.C. They planned their first date for the following weekend.

Friday afternoon Tim paid his last respects. Dan rendered a brief but soulful eulogy while struggling to suppress his gloom. After the service Tim chatted with Sheri's family, catching up on all that had transpired over the years. He shook his head at the bittersweet thought that it too often takes a tragedy to reunite relatives and old friends. Kneeling in front of Sheri's urn, Tim prayed for a brighter future. Intuition hinted that Sheri's spirit would be guiding him every step of the way.

Beneath a crisp moon the cramped flight arrived at Reagan National. Early the next morning Tim was well into his seminar. To his students he must have seemed distant, for as he rattled on about basic income capitalization, images from his youth beckoned like children's whispers. By the close of his session, he realized he'd have to visit his old neighborhood. Tim glanced at his wrist. "Plenty of time," he muttered. His flight wasn't due to depart until evening.

Tim hopped into his rental and rolled south via the interstate. It seemed as if an eternity had passed since he set foot in Seminary Valley. As he cruised through he noticed how little things had changed. The streets were as wide as he remembered; and though the sidewalks had darkened with age and the trees and bushes were overgrown, everything seemed as if he had never left. Reaching his old home Tim slowed to a crawl. He pictured gazing out his bedroom window at the wondrous moon and stars, fantasizing about his future. Tim yenned for his childhood: the thrill of youth through a fresh set of emotions and the love and understanding faithfully administered by his parents; yet most of all he craved the friendship and dreams he and Sheri shared. He could only imagine what their future together would have been like.

Continuing up the block past the homes of his former neighbors, Tim wallowed in nostalgia. He parked opposite a side yard: the route they used to get to the willow tree. A wistful smile parted his lips as he let down the windows and savored the autumn air—inviting, enticing. He had departed the intense subway of life for the tranquil carousel of his past. Thought and emotion mellowed to a warm glow. Spellbound he ogled the radiant yards until he pictured himself frolicking on the lollipop-green grass. He was ten, running and jumping and doing cartwheels with Sheri and Robert, having a blast! He wondered if the hereafter would in any way resemble this. Maybe, on his way to the next world, he'd revisit this childhood sanctuary and relive his greatest memories.

Scanning the vacant street, Tim stepped out and sauntered to his destination. His eyes twinkled. The trunk had grown tall and fat, but its velvety branches remained. Cool chills like sprinkles of spring rain prickled his scalp as he recalled the joy he and his best friends savored while nestled in the cradle of the willow. Tim yearned for a stitch of memorabilia: the flashlight they read their stories with, or Sheri's charm bracelet—even Honey's leash. He examined the tree trunk. Robert might have scrawled a message before moving to Pittsburgh . . . there was nothing. He gazed at the ground half-expecting he'd see a pool of melted vanilla ice cream oozing from a soggy cone, or maybe Robert's voodoo dolls fiercely grimacing; but no, nothing—no use pretending. Yet a vague sensation nudged him. He relaxed and surrendered to it.

Hopping behind the wheel Tim headed back past his old home. He wondered what its present owners and their kids were like. Turning onto Taney Avenue he followed it a few blocks and stopped at the crest of the hill. Thick gangly pines enveloped the front of Robert's former home, so it took a moment to picture how it used to look; yet inside there once lived a lonely, unstable child: a peculiar playmate with whom Tim had forged a sincere friendship, an innocent dreamer who had somehow morphed into a merciless maniac. To murder his parents, and the heinous manner in which he did . . . if Tim only knew why.

Instinctively he pulled onto Latham Street. He couldn't shake the feeling he was being drawn to something profound. Coasting to the bottom he parked next to the woods, which to his relief hadn't been replaced by new housing developments. The land looked untouched, unspoiled. He hopped out and headed past the dead end until he spotted the creek. Tim remembered years ago spying on Robert near the water's edge, hoping Robert would lead him to his hideout. The flow of the creek had always reminded Tim of an olive-green python slithering through a jungle. As he gazed, intuition propelled him back to his car and to the path between Latham Street and the nearby shopping center. So often he had skipped along the edge of these woods, opposite the backs of homes, on his way to the drugstore for some candy, baseball cards, or the latest monster model he couldn't wait to paint and assemble.

"Whaaa—" Tim blinked at the ground. Half covered by leaves lay a rusty saw and shovel. Robert might have used implements like these to build his fort. But did it exist? What was it Sheri said? He closed his eyes straining to recall their last conversation. Her maternal voice emerged:

"Let me see, if I remember correctly, Robert told me it was off of Latham Street—now it's coming to me—near the bottom of Latham, on the left where the woods are, at the edge of a clearing, I think."

If the clearing was still recognizable, and he uncovered Robert's hideout, something there might explain Robert's fiendish behavior.

Tim raced to his car and pocketed the mini flashlight from his briefcase. His pulse soared as he paced to the center of the woods. Everything had grown. There were twice as many trees, all in dazzling colors, yet many had long stretches of ivy running up their trunks, a strange sight. An image four yards ahead made him flinch: the remnants of a campsite for vagrants. There were weather-eaten mattresses, dirty blankets, TV dinner boxes, and empty beer cans. By day these vagabonds probably panhandled at the shopping center, but after sundown this was their spot.

Tim moved on, and then he saw it and ran to it—yes! He remembered as a boy that it was bulldozed earth. Now it brimmed with soft bluegrass. Where it joined the woods it rolled to lower ground. Aside from the creek bank, the edge of the clearing was the only spot that seemed hilly enough to burrow. He looked at how much ground he'd have to inspect. "Damn!" he scoffed. It was getting late.

Like rummaging through a crate of toys from your childhood, in search of a lost keepsake, or clearing out junk in the basement: something inevitably slows you down. A forgotten treasure pops up and you're spellbound. The more you stare at it, the more you reminisce, and before you know it you wonder how it's two hours later than when you started. He was pissing away priceless time, but it wasn't too late.

Tim scanned the edge of the clearing for anything unusual, a mound of dirt, an opening. He focused on the slope, surveying it like he would a historic commercial property, calculating the most logical place to dig for the hidden entrance. Maybe unearthing Robert's fort wasn't Tim's kismet. It probably wasn't real to begin with, or if it was, by now it had been demolished. A piece of rug barely visible beneath a patch of weeds glistened.

"Holy—" Tim gasped, his heart revving. But what would he dig with? The image of the rusty shovel at the edge of the woods beckoned.

On the brink of discovering Robert's hideout was like a touch of Christmas: the radiant glow of the wrapped presents, and guessing how many would be duds; or maybe they'd all be knock-outs—nah, but just one awesome gift was worth the wait!

Tim shoveled swiftly and within seconds a hole appeared. The November rain had been slight, yet sufficient so that the earth hospitably gave way. Minutes later the opening was large enough to access. Tim quivered at the thought of what might be inside: a rat, or snake, or rotting corpse! Who knows whom Robert had left there?

"Caw!"

Tim cocked his head as a stout crow fluttered by. The sun pierced his eyes.

"This is bullshit." He shook his fists. "Get in there and search the damn place!"

Yanking out his flashlight he squirmed into the hole and fired. Carpet remnants covered the entire area. Tim recalled that Robert's father owned a carpet franchise. Grateful his nose was stuffed up, Tim caught the slightest whiff of mildew. The hollow could accommodate four or five people. You could sit easily, but to stand you'd have to be slightly taller than a munchkin, though it was fine for Robert as an adolescent.

A vague sentiment, perhaps conjured by Robert's spirit, intimated that Tim was on sacred ground. Was he sorry Robert had endured a miserable existence? Tim was still angry at Robert for trying to kill him, and perplexed as to why he had murdered his parents. Would he ever forgive him for strangling and mutilating Sheri?

Tim shook himself and glared at the walls—nothing but carpet. "Screw it; why isn't there anything here?" He kicked a wall. For the effort he spent finding the place, the least he could do was check for bumps (things under the carpet) or perhaps an alcove with, or secret passage to, Robert's personal stash. Tim searched for a few minutes and was about to leave when he butted the ceiling. A shaggy object slapped his check. Tim screamed as he anticipated the chomp from a grisly rodent. The gleam from his flashlight struck a nebulous image that dangled at the end of a rubber strand inches from his face. It must have been wedged between the carpet strips overhead, and when he bumped it, it popped out. As Tim analyzed the relic Robert had so dearly cherished, a sinister realization made his hair stand on end: Sheri's hair—the color and texture matched. Just as Robert had stated in his letter, he had tightly sewn (to the top of John—his keepsake) strands from the mound he had discovered at Sheri's parent's house. Tim glanced at its face and cringed. It reminded him of Freddy Krueger from *A Nightmare on Elm Street*. Tim was tempted to chuck it, but when he pictured Sheri's hair, he pocketed the shrunken head wondering what Dan and Burke would say about it. Tim contemplated Robert stroking its hair. Robert must have been here sometime after he escaped from the hospital, but prior to his arrival in Seattle; though why would he leave the head? Perhaps he forgot it and planned to return after his Seattle spree. Just the thought of Robert so recently occupying this spot gave Tim goose bumps. Though Robert was dead and couldn't physically harm Tim, dark shadows invite strange notions. He needed fresh air—but wait! Tim's heart fluttered as he glimpsed the black bag tucked in the back left corner. He yanked it out and blinked. The initials R & J zapped his eyes . . . from his adolescence Tim pictured Bish and his cronies in the high school cafeteria wondering about R & J. So this *was* Robert's bag—and heavy. "I wonder—" Tim shook it and unsnapped the top flap. "Ahhh!" He dropped the bag and shivered as an ivory colored skull tumbled out. Robert must have polished it to perfection, it glistened so. Tim's hands trembled as he examined it and wondered: whose corpse had it come from? And assuming it was one of Robert's victims, what had motivated Robert to commit this murder? So the incident Tim overheard years ago at Hammond High wasn't fiction. He was stunned at the probability that Robert's mayhem dated from his childhood. Tim pitched the bag and scrambled to get out. Something clattered. "What the——" His pulse soared as he flipped over a strip of carpet . . . and there it was, a gray aluminum box. He stared in awe; wonder eclipsed trepidation. Fumbling with the latch, he tried to stay calm. "Damn, locked!"

Tim dove outside, retrieved the shovel, and returned. He pried the sides, working his way to the front until bang! The lid popped open to a curious sight. As he pondered the contents, a poignant tune like muted bells from an antique music box jingled in his head: the theme from the movie *To Kill a Mockingbird*, used at the beginning, as the box of trinkets from the tree hollow is displayed, and at the end, when Scout walks Boo—the dreaded, mysterious recluse who saves her life—home.

A large pocketknife and sharpening stone were the first mementos Tim plucked from the box. The knife was drawn. Bits of cottony fluff were matted to the blade and stone by something that resembled dried chocolate. Tim laid the implements beside the box, reached in, and clasped a faded top to a pint of Briggs vanilla ice cream. He mused over Robert's penchant for vanilla until he remembered the missing pint in his freezer. The imaginary music stopped. He dropped the top, peered into the box, and flinched. A bizarre vision flooded his eyes. More cottony fluff, like cottage cheese, covered two small, pillowy figures—click . . . the remains of Robert's voodoo dolls, mock creations of his mother and father. Though the heads were still intact, the shredded bodies dangled by threads. Dried chocolate covered each tattered doll's groin. Tim chucked them aside and shook himself. The irrepressible malevolence that had fueled the destruction of the dolls had swelled in Robert, over the years, to psychotic rage.

Tim removed a small jar of Vaseline and a 5x8 glossy of Sheri. There were stains on the photo—obvious to Tim what Robert had been up to. Tim wondered how Robert had obtained it. As he gazed at Sheri's image, his eyes watered. Dressed in tight denim shorts and a billowy blouse, she looked about 13. You could tell from her expression that she wasn't aware she was being photographed. It was as if Robert had snapped the shot while sitting in a tree.

Wiping his eyes, Tim started to repack the box when he glimpsed an audio cassette. It was Day-Glow green with speckles that resembled dried blood; no writing that he could see. Who knew what was recorded on it, maybe the screams of Robert's victims, maybe his parents' screams, how morbid. Yet the tape spiked Tim's curiosity. His heart surged as he secured the box—but wait. Behind the box was a wad of paper. Tim held his breath as he carefully unfolded the sheets. The handwriting was similar to the flowery style of Robert's letter.

Dear Tim,

Help me—HELP ME!

Things are happening that I don't understand. Please come back; I need you! I've felt cravings for some time, and I don't know how much longer I can control myself. The world is changing; I feel it and I realize, no matter how I try, I'll never fit in, it's useless. I'm beginning to hate everyone.

Today I turned fourteen. It's the summer of '69, a rotten year with no end in sight. Outside there's beauty—inside there's insanity! I've wanted so badly to tell you what's eating me. I have to tell someone, someone who won't judge me or run away. I can tell you now because you're not here staring at me like I was a lunatic, even though you're the only one who seems to understand me. But that no longer matters; I must tell you the truth. Last night, Mother and Father told me we're moving to Pittsburgh. I pleaded with them, but they said that we had no choice. I wanted to pulverize them. I can't move away: Sheri's here and there's my hideout; I worked so hard on it—I can't leave it behind! Why don't they understand? And you, you deserted me—bastard! Why did you move away? I needed you. How could you betray me? After you left, he started to take over: the bold, the wicked, the perverted Robert who's seeping into my woodwork. Maybe I should thank you for leaving because the new me is finally finding freedom, like being reborn, you know, like Frankenstein; and the more energy I gain, the more I won't be able to tolerate you, though you're not the only one. Miserable people like you deserve company. Speaking of Miss High and Mighty, Miss Too Good to Love Me: Sheri will never understand how much I care for her . . . if she only knew. The things I've done to her in my dreams would make your brain squirm.

I used to be afraid, at night, wondering what would happen. I hated myself, but now things are different. I'm settling it with the fiend inside; and once I finalize it I know I'll do something incredible.

You and Sheri and Mother and Father: I used to trust everyone. Someday I'll put an end to all the memories; then I'll be at peace. I may have to kill everyone I thought I loved—everyone I thought loved me.

I wish you really knew me; you would have helped, but I never told you my fatal secrets: I couldn't; I swore I wouldn't. Now, I can't keep things to myself any longer.

Tim, three weeks have passed. It's the beginning of August and I'm now a full-fledged monster; I've committed my first atrocity—yes! What a masterpiece of mayhem, and I was never suspected: the creeps that took the fall will I'm sure pay dearly behind bars; then, if they're ever released, I'll finish them. Their initial mistake, almost two years ago, was finding and playing with the severed head—I'll explain that later. As if that wasn't enough, no, they had to press further. You see, I was spying on them a week ago; they were drinking and toking, having the time of their lives. I wore rubber gloves and was playing with my new toy until the leader decided to venture too close to my hideout. He finished peeing when I pummeled him from behind with my knife. On the third blow I yanked down and let go, certain his friends would leave plenty of fingerprints on the handle. As I departed I commandeered the cassette player they left as they rushed to aid their comrade who was sputtering for help. I smiled. I was happy. Finally there was true order and peace in my world.

As for the severed head: You never knew my father's brother, Uncle John, and what happened a week before I told you and Sheri that crazy dream. As a matter of fact, Tim, you asked me that night, after hearing the dream, about the stranger who used to visit me; and I denied ever having a visitor. I couldn't tell you then, but now . . .

Uncle John lived three blocks away. He was older than Father, retired, and a widower. Father had warned him never to visit again. That was after he caught John feeling me. Mother, who had always been suspicious of him, was furious. Father marched him outside and swore that if he ever saw him within a block of me, he'd tear him to pieces.

Before that, John was the greatest. He always bought me gifts, you know, like the horror books and monster models I showed you. All I had to do was to say that I liked something, and the next time I saw him he'd give it to me. I also grew to love his favorite ice cream, vanilla. He'd come over and drive me to the ice cream parlor, then we'd cruise the neighborhood enjoying every lick. That was when Father trusted him. We also used to fish at the creek. Though we rarely caught anything, John bought me a large bait and tackle bag, which he inscribed with our initials, R & J. You thought my stories were great? Uncle John told me most of them, plus he taught me how to tell a good story. Sitting next to him with our bamboo poles outstretched and lunch tucked in my fishing bag, he'd pat me on the head, smile, stroke my knee, and tell me his latest adventure. Occasionally he'd fall into a trance. I'd ask him what was up, and he'd smile, glimpse the sky, and chant "Nothing, nothing's wrong—" You remember, Tim; I always used to say it; I still say it; that's because it reminds me of how great he was.

I remember, months after John felt me, Father was on the phone telling John that it didn't matter whether he had successfully completed therapy, he was never again allowed to visit. For a while everything seemed normal and good; and even though I missed John and his presents, Father would bring home gifts, plus he'd always make sure the freezer was stocked with plenty of vanilla ice cream. Anyways, it was October and it was Saturday. I was upstairs playing the Voodoo Doll Game. . . . It's so hard to tell you. I promised I wouldn't tell anyone, but ———

That was it: the letter had abruptly ended. Tim flipped over the sheets—nothing on the backs. He checked and rechecked the ground, tossing carpet everywhere. "Damn it!" He growled. "How could he just stop? I can only imagine what happened. That's not good enough. Screw it all!" Tim scrambled from the hole, thoroughly pissed.

Chapter 16

As the sun set, Tim departed the wistful recesses of Seminary Valley. He would never forget his childhood: the incredible fun with Robert and Sheri, the amazing stories, and the willow tree, which he was happy to find standing. Tim ruminated about the cassette and why he hadn't found the cassette player. Robert had probably taken it with him or trashed it. "What the hell." He stopped by Sears at Landmark Mall and purchased a portable CD boom box with cassette player, plus batteries and a set of headphones. As he headed for his flight, he listened. The tape, decades old, thumped. Was it broken? Tim held his breath until a voice rippled: nervous and frightened, the childish cadence embedded in Tim's subconscious for decades . . .

"I have to tell someone—I can't hold back any longer; and so now, the day before we leave for Pittsburgh, I'll tell it to my cassette recorder: let it be the world, the judge, and the jury for all I care; it would never betray me like certain people. Maybe years from now someone will find this tape and give it to the authorities. Then justice will be served."

Tim's heart pitched with anticipation. "Please!" He gasped.

It was as if Tim were listening for the first time to Robert's most amazing tale. His inimitable tone, texture, modulation, and the uncanny mimicry he injected into each character's voice vaulted Tim to his past, to the willow tree, and to being spellbound. But if Robert's account was true—and why shouldn't it be—then this stark declaration would be a grisly bombshell! Chills whistled through Tim in mournful tribute to what might be the moral reprieve for Robert's infamous misdeeds. As Robert pressed further Tim imagined he was in Robert's house, Robert's head, Robert's soul . . .

"The late September afternoon beckons outside my window. How I love fall: the air, the leaves, my books, my Voodoo Doll game. The house is quiet except for the clock on my dresser, 'tick tick.' Father will be home any minute; and when Mother returns from shopping, she'll cook a nice, meaty dinner. Maybe I'll go downstairs and grab a snack. I can hear my heart. It sounds nice. My body tingles. Wait, someone's coming up the walk. It must be Father. Racing to the door I unlock it and—

"'Hello Robert, it's been awhile. How are you? I've missed you.'

"'Uncle John? You're not supposed to be here.' I love Uncle John, even though there's something wrong with him.

I feel mixed up when I think of him. If Father were home he'd explode.

"'Robert, I know I shouldn't be here, but I need you to understand that what I did was an accident. I'm sorry. I'd never hurt you. Do you believe me?'

"'Yes, but you have to leave!' I push him away.

"'Here, Robert. I brought this especially for you. I won it at a carnival—my way of saying how sorry I am if I hurt you. Please keep it. It will remind you of me.'

"For a moment I'm speechless. It's the most beautiful thing I've ever seen, dangling from a string, spinning 'round and 'round. I have to grab it, run my thumb over its prune-like face, stroke its long shaggy hair, and slide it in my shirt pocket.

"'Thank you, Uncle John, but Father said—'

"'Robert, this is my last visit. I promise.' Wrapping his firm arms around me, he squeezes. 'Forgive me, Robert, please?'

"'Uncle John, you have to go—now!'

"The front door bursts open.

"'Father?'

"'John, you bastard! I warned you. Robert, upstairs— quickly!' Father snatches the steely letter opener from the hall table and glares.

"'But Father—'

"'To your room, Son!' He shoves John into the den.

"I race up until I hear the shouting.

"'Richard, I swear I was just—'

"'Damn you!'

"Yells echo, fists pop, the floor and walls shake . . . heavy breathing—silence.

"'Father, are you okay? Father?'

"His strained eyes appear. 'I'm fine. Please, do as you're told. I'll be up soon.'

"'What about John?'

"'He's fine. He'll be leaving in a minute. Now get to your room.'

"I run upstairs and leap into bed. The front door slams shut.

"'Good riddance, John.' Father's voice reverberates . . . and then his face appears. 'You all right, Son? Did he touch you or do anything bad?'

"'No, Father, nothing.'

"Father looks long and hard at me. 'Robert, I want to talk to you about everything that happened, but I must finish a project in the basement, something the carpet store needs, it won't take long. I promise, as soon as it's done and I drop it off, I'll be back and we'll have a long talk, all right?'

"'Yes, Father.'

"'Stay in your room until I return. If your mother comes home after I leave, tell her I'll be home soon. Please stay put until I return.'

"I nod, turn on my radio, pull out my new shrunken head, and fall asleep. It's a short nap, though I remember bees humming for awhile. When I awake everything is quiet except for the faint static from my portable. The green dial glows peacefully in the shadows. Twilight has arrived. I click on the table lamp and smile at the cover of my favorite paperback, *Vulture's Stew*—I love being at home. Bouncing from my bed I enter the hall. 'Mother . . . Father . . . anyone here?' I skip downstairs to their room. Everything looks right, feels right: the tie rack, the dresser, the picture of Mother and Father, and the bed; Father bought it because it reminded him of Ebenezer Scrooge's in *A Christmas Carol*. Mother approved.

"In the kitchen I open the bread box and eat a slice. What has Father been working on? Maybe he left a drawing of it downstairs. Funny, the lights in the cellar won't come on, but I do have my penlight. Better be quick: Mother or Father will be home soon. Slinking downstairs I flip the other switch . . . nothing. Turning the corner I click on my pen-light and shiver—Father's prized possession, the painting of the clipper ship battered against the rocky shore. It rouses my earliest childhood memory, our trip to the beach. The beach wasn't the problem, it was the ocean. I wasn't ready the first time Father tried to teach me to swim. He didn't understand how frightened I was of the waves. He thought if he threw me in I'd eventually learn to be a great swimmer, 'just like the Viking children,' he said. I kicked and screamed, but it didn't matter. Mother was fixing lunch. The tide was high, the water, freezing, the waves—monstrous! I was seconds from drowning when Father realized. He pulled me out, cradled me, and told me how much he loved me. He promised he'd never again force me to do anything like that, but it was too late; the damage was done.

"I quickly pass Father's painting and enter his workroom. Something putrid reeks. From the gleam of my penlight, the far wall holds Father's hardware: hacksaws, drills, hammers, and chisels. There are gaps where certain tools are missing. I can only wonder. As I pull away, the huge teeth of Father's circular saw glare, and from the machine a dark swill dribbles to the floor. 'Mother, Father—anyone home?' Terrified, I bolt to the stairs, then turn and halt. The enormous freezer chest pulsates in the distance. Like a deep-sea diver I lumber to it. Why can't I escape? I feel strapped in on a giant roller coaster creeping up the first hill, the metal gears bumping and grinding. You rise so high you wonder whether you can stand the fall, as if someone tossed you from a jet over the vortex of a seething ocean. The chest is barely open. It calls to me, and from its depths I realize my life will forever change. Holding my breath I thrust open the lid, fan the stench, and scream: 'No, God, Please!' I can't stop screaming. It's too insane to be real. The jumbled, rotting pieces of flesh have an identity; and from his mouth protrude his genitals; and from his battered, severed head is the face of my Uncle John. I reel before hitting the floor. Someone shakes me awake.

"'Robert—you all right?'

"From the upstairs hall Mother shouts, 'Richard, please bring him here.'

"They talk and talk; will they ever stop making excuses. Father tells me how John was responsible for his actions and that Father had to make sure John would never again bother me.

Uncle John gave him no choice. I explain how much I love John and that I believe he changed. That's when Mother tells me that I mustn't think that way. Father has done this to protect me, and we have to as a family stick together. No one must know. They reason, then plead until I agree never to tell, but only if I can continue to see Tim and Sheri, at least occasionally.

"I almost forgot: late Saturday night, about four weeks after John's death, I snuck out to the back porch with a snack. I was gazing at the moon when a piercing scream jolted me. I nearly dropped my dish of ice cream. I was sure the cry came from the woods. I waited to make sure Father and Mother did not wake; then I tore down Latham Street and into the woods, following the creek, stealthily moving towards something that sounded like teenagers. As I reached the group I heard one of them tell the others to be quiet. I held my breath hoping they wouldn't spot me. Eventually they vacated, and I hopped down the creek bank to what they left behind . . . my bait and tackle bag and Uncle John's head. Someone had removed the genitals, probably Father because I don't believe the teens would have the stomach to touch them. Father, after placing the head in the bag, must have tossed it into the creek near the sewer; the rains probably carried it downstream, dumping it onto the creeks' edge. I wanted to kill Father, but that would wait. I had to find a place to store the head—my hide out, of course.

"Boy you should have seen me when the police questioned us about John's disappearance. I acted as if I hadn't a clue what was going on. I was a natural. Whatever, it worked and I continued to see Sheri, and also Tim—until he moved; then Father and Mother, because of the so called 'accident,' thought it best that we move to Pittsburgh. After begging and threatening, I caved in and agreed to go. But don't worry, I'll get my revenge.

Robert drifted for a moment. He started chanting a song: its whimsical poetry and hypnotic melody reminded Tim of the mid-sixties hit, *Pretty Ballerina*, by the Left Banke. His adolescent voice, whispering the lyrics, gave Tim chills. He pictured Robert singing it to Sheri, trying so hard to win her love:

SO BRILLIANT YOUR GAZE, YOU SOAR TO MY LIGHT
SO RADIANT TO ME, MY SPARROW IN FLIGHT
"SHALL WE?" I SMILE, YOU NOD, WE DANCE
FAR YONDER WE JET, DIVINE, ENTRANCED

There was 10 seconds of dead space . . . The tape hissed like a cornered cobra. Robert's voice finally reemerged: a tight whisper. He strained and wheezed as he desperately regurgitated his words. It was as if someone were beating the crap out of him, yet Tim felt sure Robert was alone when he made the tape. Robert exploded:

"Mother, Father, you say you love me, but you won't help. You never help—damn you! Uncle John was my best friend. He loved me. I know he made a mistake, but all he wanted was forgiveness. Murderers, cowards, you make me sick. The only decent thing to do is to rip your bloody guts out like this!"

The fierce pounding pummeled Tim's eardrums, and then he pictured it. Robert was stabbing his voodoo dolls, screaming in agony as he disgorged every inch of pent-up rage. Tim had never heard anything like it. Robert's intense emotion was heartbreaking. Tim swerved into a nearby lot and nosed for the shade of an overlapping tree. Jerking the keys from the ignition, he buried his face in his hands. Robert screamed and wept. His cries raked Tim's head and heart. With each phrase, Robert stabbed one doll, then the other.

I HATE YOU, MOTHER! I HATE YOU, FATHER!
MOTHER-WHORE-BITCH!
FATHER-SCUM-BASTARD!
KILL YOU, MOTHER! KILL YOU FATHER!
I HATE YOU ALL!
HATE! HATE! HATE! HATE! HAAEEEEEET!

Tim's chest surged. He went completely flush. Tears welled from his swollen cheeks as he spewed everything that for ages had been locked inside of him. He cried like a frightened child. He cried as if he had lost everything that had ever mattered. He cried hard and long. Oh how he pitied Robert.

For the next few minutes Tim listened carefully to the hiss. He fast-forwarded the tape, but nothing. He flipped the cassette over, still nothing. Ejecting the tape, he tucked it in his shirt pocket. This was too personal too lose. Maybe he'd burn it . . . nah!

As Tim started his car he glimpsed something. "Wha——" he gasped. Robert's metal box had tumbled to the floor and flipped upside down. Stuck to the bottom was a mesmerizing photo. Tim pulled the faded 5x8 from the box and gazed with awe. Unbelievable, yet there they were, side by side, smiling and carefree. Tim's memory of Uncle John was incredibly accurate: the slicked back hair, horn-rimmed glasses, ivory colored button-down shirt, charcoal cardigan, and wool slacks. Robert's father must have taken the picture. Robert and John stood in front of the rear of John's 'Valiant waving to the camera, having the time of their lives. Between them, hand painted below the trunk emblem, where the words:

Fatal Dreams

Tim began piecing together the hollow spots of his life. When he first moved to Seattle, he had subconsciously blamed himself for not spending enough time with Robert, or at least not trying to help Robert overcome his neurotic hang-ups. However, after listening to the cassette, Tim realized there was little he or anyone could have done unless perhaps Robert had divulged the truth about John's demise. A gust of relief soothed Tim. The subtle yet substantial guilt of leaving Robert for Seattle waned. Though he detested Robert's actions Tim could at least, from the mitigating nature of Robert's baneful motives, feel sympathy. Tim considered his vital relationships. It seemed as if everyone he loved had somehow slipped through his fingers. He pictured himself as Errol Flynn in gleaming regalia on horseback thrusting his sword and screaming "Onward men!" Into the valley of death rode the six hundred—cannons to the left, cannons to the right—all Tim's comrades and loved ones crashing, burning, dropping to the guns—the Charge of the Light Brigade—the charge of his friends and lovers to their deaths! He lost Sheri through carelessness, then to Dan, and then to Robert. Maureen exited with drugs. As for Robert: his father's transgressions set the wheel in motion, and Dan tore it to pieces. Why had almost everyone Tim truly cared about departed? Was it a training ground for a better future? Everything had to have a purpose, didn't it? Before her death Tim was oblivious to Maureen's true nature; yet when she died he wanted to pulverize all the wretched evil of the world—it was the enemy. Struggling with Maureen and her heroin overdose was like so many of his struggles with life's obscenities, which he could continue to ignore by reveling inside the carefree womb of his past and classic movies, and lulling himself with his fantasies and rationalizations of people; but when would it end? Dealing with reality as an adult was often awkward and painful. For years Tim was trapped, a slave to his memories and daydreams because the past seemed idyllic. Yet an inner force incited him to a better way of coping with reality, which he needed because, as euphoric as his memories seemed, reveling in them deprived him of the challenges and joys of living in the present.

With the death of Sheri and Robert, Tim's illusions of the past, like a snow covered field beneath a July sun, quickly melted. His beloved childhood friends were freeing him from his nostalgic citadel, the sentimental refuge that had alienated him from reality. It was time to abandon the imaginary: to open up and accept people for who they truly are—not by first impressions; to appreciate the present, enjoying and living in it as ardently as he had enjoyed and lived in the past; and to welcome the future.

As for April, things could work out. Up to now he had been fortunate with his career, beliefs, and standard of living; though he still lacked perhaps the most vital asset, a loving mate who would care for him as he would for her. With April he would be complete. He yearned for her. "Fate, bring me happiness!"

Robert was singing in Tim's head . . . more lines from his concocted song.

FOR YOU ARE BEAUTY THAT BLAZES ME BLIND
A DREAM SO DEAR, FOR ME YOU SHALL DIE
FOR ME YOU SHALL DIE

Tim's voice faded to tears.

EPILOGUE

Day, sun, light, warmth, clear blue sky, thick trees, rich grass—sweet earth! He loves it all . . . almost as much as he loves her.

Laughing and splashing, cool water, the smell of suntan lotion and chlorine, the patter of bare feet, girls in bikinis and one-pieces, guys in baggy trunks with brilliant splashes of color—some with their hair done up like a thousand needles. The whistle blows to let the younger kids back in. From the midst pops the grind of something modern yet primitive. Tim swears it's from the mid-sixties, but no. Sharp jabs from a keyboard, the thud from a bass drum, and a voodoo rhythm, blaze with the torch of a human voice. Mumbo-jumbo lyrics spark ears and burst into fireballs of poetry, which cool to a crisp chorus. The song wanes . . . tranquility.

In the distance, overlooking it all, on a hill, under life's most radiant orb, he's beside her. His eyes twinkle to the golden rays that glisten from her hair, her eyes, her supple skin, her carefree smile—profile of beauty, his love.

A new sound completes the picture: a sweet voice caressing the air with an angelic melody. And in her lyrics is a plea for salvation. This is their song. Something about it makes them glow.

They've been together for months; they've made profound, intense love; in their own way they've committed to one another. He's never felt so whole. They caress and kiss, effervescing with love. A moment later she parts the silence:

"I can't believe we've come this far. It seems like yesterday I was taking care of you at the hospital. And now . . . I can't imagine being with anyone like I am with you."

"To me," he smiles as though he's at the entrance of Shangri-La, "you are everything. I've found my home."

They embrace and nestle.

"Over the past months we've realized so much about each other, but——" she sighs.

He remains silent.

"You never told me everything: what happened just before we met at the hospital. I thought I'd give you time to think it through." She squeezes his shoulders.

"I have put it off. It's a long story." He probes her eyes. "Are you sure you want to hear it? It may take hours."

"I have time," she smiles.

"Well . . ."

Though he has ceased imagining her as his childhood sweet-heart, the look on her face reminds him of a nine-year-old waiting patiently for dessert. She is here now and will no doubt remain with him for the rest of his life. He loves her for who she is. He has found peace. He no longer aches for the past. The chains of nostalgia have parted. They gaze at one another knowing that their life, a far better life unfettered by the past, has just begun.

FROM THE AUTHOR

I grew up in Seminary Valley, a suburb within the city limits of Alexandria, Virginia. I'm happy to report that Seminary Valley appears as it always has, not including slight home and city improvements and the growth of trees and shrubs, etc.

ACKNOWLEDGEMENTS

For their facts and observations—which are vital to story detail and timeframe, much of which is set in the late 1960s—and for their kindness and inspiration, my sincere appreciation goes to my wife, the Lennhoffs, relatives, and: Matt Albers, Brian Anderson, Kathleen Baker, Jeff Bean, Kevin Bishop, Pete Bloodgood, Bob and Rita Bogardus, Paul Brown, Don Burke, Ed Catterall, Dick Cline, Richard Downey, Mark Fordenbacher, Rusty Gibson, Joe Grigg, Tim Heberling, Denise Henderson, Greg Holmes, Hal Horstman, Pam and Moses Hull, Ed Humphreys, Gary Johnson, Pam Kachur, Jon and BettyJo Matzinger Lash, Dave and Sue Lay, Al Leary, Mark Madden, Mike Mazujian, Mike McGowan, Elizabeth Mechling, Valerie Myer, Frank Palladino, Tom Perry, Bruce Pilch, Dave and Sarah Purol, Dan Reznikov, Ray Rollins, Chris Rothe, Matt Staszak, Rene Thierry, Rob White, Peter Wolman, and Damon Woods.

Thank you!

Drew Landreth is a native of Northern Virginia and a former member of Washington Independent Writers. Fatal Dreams is his first novel. Other works in progress include three novels, a book of short stories, and poetry. Drew is also a composer, songwriter, singer and guitarist. His daytime employment background is in banking and real estate appraisal.

69846619R00120

Made in the USA
Columbia, SC
24 April 2017